TWO LITTLE PILGRIMS' PROGRESS

MRS. BURNETT'S FAMOUS JUVENILES.

PICCINO, AND OTHER CHILD STORIES.

SQUARE 8vo, $1.50.

" The history of Piccino's ' two days ' is as delicate as one of the anemones that spring in the rock walls facing Piccino's Mediterranean—a study rather than a story of child-life. . . . The other stories in the book have the charm of their predecessor in material and manner. . . . A delightful volume, in fair print, and furthermore embellished by Mr. Birch's graceful and sympathetic drawings."—MRS. BURTON HARRISON.

LITTLE LORD FAUNTLEROY.

SQUARE 8vo, $2.00.

"In 'Little Lord Fauntleroy' we gain another charming child to add to our gallery of juvenile heroes and heroines: one who teaches a great lesson with such truth and sweetness that we part with him with real regret when the episode is over."—LOUISA M. ALCOTT.

SARA CREWE.

SQUARE 8vo, $1.00.

" Everybody was in love with ' Little Lord Fauntleroy,'' and I think all the world and the rest of mankind will be in love with 'Sara Crewe.' The tale is so tender, so wise, so human, that I wish every girl in America could read it, for I think everyone would be made better by it."— LOUISE CHANDLER MOULTON.

GIOVANNI AND THE OTHER.
CHILDREN WHO HAVE MADE STORIES.

SQUARE 8vo, $1.50.

Four of these stories, sad, sweet and touched with delicate humor, are about little Italian waifs who crept into the author's heart. Two of the stories are of incidents in the lives of Mrs. Burnett's own boys; and the others, while varied in subject, have the same magic charm of disclosing the beauty of child-life with a sympathy and warmth of feeling the secret of which Mrs. Burnett alone seems to possess.

LITTLE SAINT ELIZABETH,
AND OTHER STORIES.

SQUARE 8vo, $1.50.

" The pretty tale has for its heroine a little French girl brought up in an old château in Normandy by an aunt who is a recluse and a devote. A child of this type transplanted suddenly to the realistic atmosphere of New York must inevitably have much to suffer. The quaint little figure blindly trying to guess the riddle of duty under these unfamiliar conditions is pathetic, and Mrs. Burnett touches it in with delicate strokes."— SUSAN COOLIDGE.

Illustrated by REGINALD B. BIRCH.

THEIR DREAM HAD COME TRUE.

Two Little Pilgrims' Progress

A STORY OF THE CITY BEAUTIFUL

BY

Frances Hodgson Burnett

NEW-YORK
CHARLES SCRIBNER'S SONS
1895

Copyright, 1895, by
CHARLES SCRIBNER'S SONS.

Press of J. J. Little & Co.
Astor Place, New York

LIST OF ILLUSTRATIONS

FROM DRAWINGS BY REGINALD B. BIRCH

TWO LITTLE PILGRIMS' PROGRESS

I

THE sun had set, and the shadows were deepening in the big barn. The last red glow—the very last bit which reached the corner the children called the Straw Parlor—had died away, and Meg drew her knees up higher, so as to bring the pages of her book nearer to her eyes as the twilight deepened, and it became harder to read. It was her bitterest grievance that this was what always happened when she became most interested and excited— the light began to fade away, and the shadows to fill all the corners and close in about her.

She frowned as it happened now—a fierce little frown which knitted her childish black brows as she pored over her book, devouring the page, with the determination to seize on as much as was possible. It was like running a desperate race with the darkness.

She was a determined child, and no one would have

failed to guess as much who could have watched her for a
few moments as she sat on her curious perch, her cheeks
supported by her hands, her shock of straight black hair
tumbling over her forehead.

The Straw Parlor was the top of a straw stack in Aunt
Matilda's barn.   Robin had discovered it one day by climb-
ing a ladder which had been left leaning against the stack,
and when he had found himself on the top of it he had
been enchanted by the feeling it gave him of being so high
above the world, and had called Meg up to share it with
him.

She had been even more enchanted than he.

They both hated the world down below—Aunt Matilda's
world—which seemed hideous and exasperating and sordid
to them in its contrast to the world they had lived in before
their father and mother had died, and they had been sent to
their sole relation, who did not want them, and only took
them in from respect to public opinion.   Three years they
had been with Aunt Matilda, and each week had seemed
more unpleasant than the last.   Mrs. Matilda Jennings was
a renowned female farmer of Illinois, and she was far too
energetic a manager and business woman to have time to
spend on children.   She had an enormous farm, and managed it herself with a success and ability which made her
celebrated in agricultural papers.   If she had not given her
dead brother's children a home, they would have starved or
been sent to the poorhouse.   Accordingly, she gave them

food to eat and beds to sleep in, but she scarcely ever had time to notice them. If she had had time to talk to them, she had nothing to say. She cared for nothing but crops and new threshing-machines and fertilizers, and they knew nothing about such things.

"She never says anything but 'Go to bed,' 'Keep out of the way.' She's not like a woman at all," Meg commented once, "she's like a man in woman's clothes."

Their father had been rather like a woman in man's clothes. He was a gentle little, slender man, with a large head. He had always been poor, and Mrs. Matilda Jennings had regarded him as a contemptible failure. He had had no faculty for business or farming. He had taught school, and married a school teacher. They had had a small house, but somehow it had been as cosey as it was tiny. They had managed to surround themselves with an atmosphere of books, by buying the cheap ones they could afford and borrowing the expensive ones from friends and circulating libraries. The twins—Meg and Robin—had heard stories and read books all the first years of their lives, as they sat in their little seats by the small, warm fireside. In Aunt Matilda's bare, cold house there was not a book to be seen. A few agricultural papers were scattered about. Meals were hurried over as necessary evils. The few people who appeared on the scene were farmers, who talked about agricultural implements and the wheat market.

"It's such a bare place," Robin used to say, and he

would drive his hands into the depths of his pockets and set his square little jaw, and stare before him.

Both the twins had that square little jaw. Neither of them looked like their father and mother, except that from their mother they inherited black hair. Robin's eyes were black, but Meg's were gray, with thick black lashes. They were handsome little creatures, but their shocks of straight black hair, their straight black brows and square little jaws, made them look curiously unlike other children. They both remembered one winter evening, when, as they sat on their seat by the fire, their father, after looking at them with a half smile for a moment or so, began to laugh.

"Margaret," he said to their mother, "do you know who those two are like? You have heard me speak of Matilda often enough."

"Oh, Robert!" she exclaimed, "surely they are not like Matilda?"

"Well, perhaps it is too much to say they are like her," he answered, "but there is something in their faces that reminds me of her strongly. I don't know what it is exactly, but it is there. It is a good thing, perhaps," with a queer tone in his voice. "Matilda always did what she made up her mind to do. Matilda was a success. I was always a failure."

"Ah, no, Bob," she said, "not a failure!"

She had put her hand on his shoulder, and he lifted it and pressed it against his thin cheek.

"Wasn't I, Maggie?" he said, gently, "wasn't I? Well, I think these two will be like Matilda in making up their minds and getting what they want."

Before the winter was over Robin and Meg were orphans, and were with Aunt Matilda, and there they had been ever since.

Until the day they found the Straw Parlor it had seemed as if no corner in the earth belonged to them. Meg slept on a cot in a woman servant's room, Robin shared a room with some one else. Nobody took any notice of them.

"When any one meets us anywhere," Meg said, "they always look surprised. Dogs who are not allowed in the house are like us. The only difference is that they don't drive us out. But we are just as much in the way."

"I know," said Robin; "if it wasn't for you, Meg, I should run away."

"Where?" said Meg.

"Somewhere," said Robin, setting his jaw; "I'd find a place."

"If it wasn't for you," said Meg, "I should be so lonely that I should walk into the river. I wouldn't stand it." It is worth noticing that she did not say "I *could* not stand it."

But after the day they found the Straw Parlor they had an abiding-place. It was Meg who preëmpted it before she had been on the top of the stack five minutes. After she had stumbled around, looking about her, she stopped short, and looked down into the barn.

"Robin," she said, "this is another world. We are miles and miles away from Aunt Matilda. Let us make this into our home—just yours and mine—and live here."

"We are in nobody's way—nobody will even know where we are," said Robin. "Nobody ever asks, you know. Meg, it will be just like our own. We will live here." And so they did. On fine days, when they were tired of playing, they climbed the ladder to rest on the heap of yellow straw; on wet days they lay and told each other stories, or built caves, or read their old favorite books over again. The stack was a very high one, and the roof seemed like a sort of big tent above their heads, and the barn floor a wonderful, exaggeratedly long, distance below. The birds who had nests in the rafters became accustomed to them, and one of the children's chief entertainments was to lie and watch the mothers and fathers carry on their domestic arrangements, feeding their young ones, and quarrelling a little sometimes about the way to bring them up. The twins invented a weird little cry, with which they called each other, if one was in the Straw Parlor and the other one entered the barn, to find out whether it was occupied or not. They never mounted to the Straw Parlor, or descended from it, if any one was within sight. This was their secret. They wanted to feel that it was very high, and far away from Aunt Matilda's world, and if any one had known where they were, or had spoken to them from below, the charm would have been broken.

This afternoon, as Meg pored over her book, she was waiting for Robin. He had been away all day. At twelve years old Robin was not of a light mind. When he had been only six years old he had had serious plans. He had decided that he would be a great inventor. He had also decided—a little later—that he would not be poor, like his father, but would be very rich. He had begun by having a savings bank, into which he put rigorously every penny that was given to him. He had been so quaintly systematic about it that people were amused, and gave him pennies instead of candy and toys. He kept a little banking book of his own. If he had been stingy he would have been a very unpleasant little boy, but he was only strict with himself. He was capable of taking from his capital to do the gentlemanly thing by Meg at Christmas.

"He has the spirit of the financier, that is all," said his father.

Since he had been with Aunt Matilda he had found opportunities to earn a trifle rather frequently. On the big place there were small, troublesome duties the farm hands found he could be relied on to do, which they were willing to pay for. They found out that he never failed them.

"Smart little chap," they said; "always up to time when he undertakes a thing."

To-day he had been steadily at work under the head man. Aunt Matilda had no objection to his odd jobs.

"He has his living to earn, and he may as well begin," she said.

So Meg had been alone since morning. She had only one duty to perform, and then she was free. The first spring they had been with Aunt Matilda Robin had invested in a few chickens, and their rigorous care of them had resulted in such success that the chickens had become a sort of centre of existence to them. They could always have any dreams of the future upon the fortune to be gained by chickens. You could calculate on bits of paper about chickens and eggs until your head whirled at the magnitude of your prospects. Meg's duty was to feed them, and show them scrupulous attentions when Robin was away.

After she had attended to them she went to the barn, and, finding it empty, climbed up to the Straw Parlor with an old "Pilgrim's Progress," to spend the day.

This afternoon, when the light began to redden and then to die away, she and Christian were very near the gates. She longed so to go in with him, and was yearning towards them with breathless eagerness, when she heard Robin's cry below, coming up from the barn floor.

She sprang up with a start, feeling bewildered a second, before she answered. The City Beautiful was such millions —such millions of miles away from Aunt Matilda's barn. She found herself breathing quickly and rubbing her eyes, as she heard Robin hurrying up the ladder.

Somehow she felt as if he was rather in a hurry, and when his small, black shock head and wide-awake black eyes appeared above the straw she had a vague feeling that he was excited, and that he had come from another world. He clambered on to the stack and made his way to her, and threw himself full length on the straw at her side.

"Meg!" he said—"Hallo, you look as if you were in a dream! Wake up!—Jones and Jerry are coming to the barn—I hurried to get here before them; they're talking about something I want you to hear—something new! Wake up!"

"Oh, Robin!" said Meg, clutching her book and coming back to earth with a sigh, "I don't want to hear Jones and Jerry. I don't want to hear any of the people down there. I've been reading the 'Pilgrim's Progress,' and I do wish—I do so *wish* there *was* a City Beautiful."

Robin gave a queer little laugh. He really was excited.

"There is going to be one," he said. "Jones and Jerry don't really know it, but it is something like that they are talking about; a City Beautiful—a real one—on this earth, and not a hundred miles away. Let's get near the edge and listen."

II

THEY drew as near to the edge as they could without being seen. They did not understand in the least. Robin was not given to practical jokes, but what he had said sounded rather as if there was a joke somewhere. But she saw Jones and Jerry enter the barn, and saw, before they entered, that they were deep in talk. It was Jones who was speaking. Jones was Aunt Matilda's head man, and was an authority on many things.

"There's been exhibitions and fairs all over the world," he was saying, "but there's been nothing like what this will be. It will be a city, that's what it will be, and all the world is going to be in it. They are going to build it fronting on the water, and bank the water up into lakes and canals, and build places like white palaces beside them, and decorate the grounds with statues and palms and flowers and fountains, and there's not a country on earth that won't send things to fill the buildings. And there won't be anything a man can't see by going through 'em. It'll be as good as a college course to spend a week there."

Meg drew a little closer to Robin in the straw.

"What are they talking about?" she whispered.

"Listen," said Bob.

Jerry, who was moving about at some work below, gave a chuckling laugh.

"Trust 'em to do the biggest thing yet, or bust, them Chicago people," he said. "It's got to be the biggest thing —a Chicago Fair."

"It's not goin' to be the Chicago Fair," Jones said. "They're not goin' to put up with no such idea as that; it's the World's Fair. They're going to ring in the universe."

"That's Chicago out an' out," said Jerry. "Buildin's twenty stories high, an' the thermometer twenty-five degrees below zero, an' a World's Fair. Christopher Columbus! I'd like to see it!"

"I bet Christopher Columbus would like to see it," said Jones. "It's out of compliment to him they're getting it up—for discovering Chicago."

"Well, I didn't know he made his name that way partic'lar," said Jerry. "Thought what he prided hisself on was discoverin' America."

"Same thing," said Jones, "same thing! Wouldn't have had much to blow about, and have statues set up, and comic operas written about him, if it had only been America he'd discovered. Chicago does him full credit, and she's goin' to give him a send-off that'll be a credit to her."

Robin smothered a little laugh in his coat-sleeve. He was quite used to hearing jokes about Chicago. The people in the country round it were enormously proud of it,

and its great schemes and great buildings and multi-million-
naires, but those who were given to jokes had the habit of
being jocular about it, just as they had the habit of pro-
claiming and dwelling upon its rush and wealth and enterprise.   But Meg was not a jocular person.   She was too
intense and easily excited.   She gave Robin an impatient
nudge with her elbow, not in reproof, but as a sort of irre-
pressible ejaculation.

"I wish they wouldn't be funny," she exclaimed.   "I
want them to tell more about it.   I wish they'd go on."

But they did not go on; at least, not in any way that
was satisfactory.   They only remained in the barn a short
time longer, and they were busy with the work they had
come to do.   Meg craned her neck and listened, but they
did not tell more, and she was glad when they went away,
so that she could turn to Robin.

"Don't you know more than that?" she said.   "Is it
true?   What have you heard?   Tell me yourself."

"I've heard a lot to-day," said Robin.   "They were
all talking about it all the time, and I meant to tell you
myself, only I saw Jones and Jerry coming, and thought,
perhaps, we should hear something more if we listened."

They clambered over to their corner and made themselves comfortable.   Robin lay on his back, but Meg leaned
on her elbows, as usual, with her cheeks resting on her
hands.   Her black elf-locks hung over her forehead, and
her big eyes shone.

"EVERYTHING IN THE WORLD," SAID ROBIN.

"Rob," she said, "go on.   What's the rest?"

"The rest!" he said.   "It would take a week to tell it all, I should think.   But it's going to be the most wonderful thing in the world.   They are going to build a place that will be like a white, beautiful city, on the borders of the lake—that was why I called it the City Beautiful.   It won't be on the top of a hill, of course——"

"But if it is on the edge of the lake, and the sun shines and the big water is blue and there are shining white palaces, it will be better, I believe," said Meg.   "What is going to be in the city?"

"Everything in the world," said Robin.   "Things from everywhere—from every country."

"There are a great many countries," said Meg.   "You know how it is in the geography.   Europe, Asia, and Africa, as well as America.   Spain and Portugal and France and England—and Sweden and Norway and Russia and Lapland—and India—and Italy—and Switzerland, and all the others."

"There will be things—and people—brought from them all.   I heard them say so.   They say there will be villages, with people walking about in them."

"Do they walk about when they are at home?" exclaimed Meg.

"Yes, in the queer clothes they wear in their own countries.   There's going to be an Esquimaux village."

"With dogs and sledges?" cried Meg, lifting her head.

"Yes ; and you know that place in Italy where the streets are made of water——"

"It's Venice," said Meg. "And they go about in boats called gondolas."

"And the men who take them about are called gondoliers," interrupted Robin. "And they have scarfs and red caps, and push their boats along with poles. There will be gondolas at the Fair, and people can get into them and go about the canals."

"Just as they do in Venice?" Meg gasped.

"Just as they do in Venice. And it will be the same with all the other countries. It will be as if they were all brought there—Spanish places and Egyptian places and German places—and French and Italian and Irish and Scotch and English—and all the others."

"To go there would be like travelling all over the world," cried Meg.

"Yes," said Rob, excitedly. "And all the trades will be there, and all the machines—and inventions—and pictures—and books—and statues—and scientific things—and wonderful things—and everything any one wants to learn about in all the world!"

In his excitement, his words had become so rapid that they almost tumbled over each other, and he said the last sentence in a rush. There were red spots on his cheeks, and a queer look in his black eyes. He had been listening to descriptions of this thing all day. A new hand, hot from

the excitement in Chicago, had been among the workers. Apparently he had heard of nothing else, thought of nothing else, talked of nothing else, and dreamed of nothing else but the World's Fair for weeks. Finding himself among people who had only bucolic and vague ideas about it, he had poured forth all he knew, and being a rather good talker, had aroused great excitement. Robin had listened with eyes and ears wide open. He was a young human being, born so full of energy and enterprise that the dull, prosaic emptiness of his life in Aunt Matilda's world had been more horrible than he had been old enough to realize. He could not have explained why it had seemed so maddening to him, but the truth was that in his small, boyish body was imprisoned the force and ability which in manhood build great schemes, and not only build, but carry them out. In him was imprisoned one of the great business men, inventors, or political powers of the new century. But of this he knew nothing, and so ate his young heart out in Aunt Matilda's world, sought refuge with Meg in the Straw Parlor, and was bitterly miserable and at a loss.

How he had drunk in every word the man from Chicago had uttered! How he had edged near to him and tried not to lose him for a moment! How he had longed for Meg to listen with him, and had hoarded up every sentence! If he had not been a man in embryo, and a strong and clear-headed creature, he would have done his work badly. But he never did his work badly. He held on like a little bull-

2

dog, and thought of what Meg would say when they sat in the straw together. Small wonder that he looked excited when his black head appeared above the edge of the straw. He was wrought up to the highest pitch. Small wonder that there were deep red spots on his cheeks, and that there was a queer, intense look in his eyes, and about his obstinate little mouth.

He threw up his arms with a desperate gesture.

"*Everything*," he said again, staring straight before him, "that any one could want to learn about—everything in all the world."

"Oh, Robin!" said Meg, in quite a fierce little voice, "and we—*we* shall never see it!"

She saw Robin clinch his hands, though he said nothing, and it made her clinch her own hands. Robin's were tough little, square-fingered fists, brown and muscular; Meg's hands were long-fingered, flexible, and slender, but they made good little fists when they doubled themselves up.

"Rob," she said, "we never see anything! We never hear anything! We never learn anything! If something doesn't happen we shall be Nothings—that's what we shall be—Nothings!" And she struck her fist upon the straw.

Rob's jaw began to look very square, but he did not speak.

"We are twelve years old," Meg went on. "We've been here three years, and we don't know one thing we didn't know when we came here. If we had been with father and

mother we should have been learning things all the time. We haven't one thing of our own, Rob, but the chickens and the Straw Parlor—and the Straw Parlor might be taken away from us."

Rob's square jaw relaxed just sufficiently to allow of a grim little grin.

"We've got the Treasure, Meg," he said.

Meg's laugh had rather a hysterical sound. That she should not have mentioned the Treasure among their belongings was queer. They talked so much about the Treasure. At this moment it was buried in an iron bank, deep in the straw, about four feet from where they sat. It was the very bank Robin had hoarded his savings in when he had begun at six years old with pennies, and a ten-cent blank-book to keep his accounts in. Everything they had owned since then had been pushed and dropped into it— all the chicken and egg money, and all Robin had earned by doing odd jobs for any one who would give him one. Nobody knew about the old iron bank any more than they knew about the Straw Parlor, and the children, having buried it in the straw, called it the Treasure. Meg's stories about it were numerous and wonderful. Sometimes magicians came, and multiplied it a hundred-fold. Sometimes robbers stole it, and they themselves gave chase, and sought it with wild adventure ; but perhaps the most satisfactory thing was to invent ways to spend it when it had grown to enormous proportions. Sometimes they bought a house

in New York, and lived there together. Sometimes they traded in foreign lands with it. Sometimes they bought land, which increased in value to such an extent that they were millionnaires in a month. Ah! it was a treasure indeed.

After the little, low, over-strained laugh, Meg folded her arms on the straw and hid her face in them. Robin looked at her with a troubled air for about a minute. Then he spoke to her.

"It's no use doing that," he said.

"It's no use doing anything," Meg answered, her voice muffled in her arms. "I don't want to do this any more than you do. We're so lonely!"

"Yes, we're lonely," said Robin, "that's a fact." And he stared up at the dark rafters above him, and at some birds who were clinging to them and twittering about a nest.

"I said I wished there was a City Beautiful," Meg said, "but it seems to make it worse that there is going to be something like it so near, and that we should never get any nearer to it than a hundred miles."

Rob sat up, and locked his hands together round his knees.

"How do you know?" he said.

"How do I know?" cried Meg, desperately, and she lifted her head, turning her wet face sideways to look at him. He unlocked his hands to give his forehead a hard

rub, as if he were trying either to rub some thought out of or into it.

"Just because we are lonely there *is* use in doing things," he said. "There's nobody to do them for us. At any rate, we've got as far on the way to the City as the bottom of the Hill of Difficulty."

And he gave his forehead another rub and looked straight before him, and Meg drew a little closer to him on the straw, and the family of birds filled the silence with domestic twitters.

III

DURING the weeks that followed they spent more time than ever, in their hiding-place. They had an absorbing topic of conversation, a new and wonderful thing, better than their old books, even better than the stories Meg made when she lay on the straw, her elbows supporting her, her cheeks on her hands, and her black-lashed gray eyes staring into space. Hers were always good stories, full of palaces and knights and robber chiefs and fairies. But this new thing had the thrill of being a fairy story which was real—so real that one could read about it in the newspapers, and everybody was talking about it, even Aunt Matilda, her neighbors, and the work-hands on the farm. To the two lonely children, in their high nest in the straw-stack, it seemed a curious thing to hear these people in the world below talk about it in their ordinary, everyday way, without excitement or awe, as if it was a new kind of big ploughing or winnowing machine. To them it was a thing so beautiful that they could scarcely find the words to express their thoughts and dreams about it, and yet they were never alone together without trying to do so.

On wet, cheerless days, in which they huddled close to-

gether in their nest to keep from being chilled, it was their comfort to try to imagine and paint pictures of the various wonders until, in their interest, they forgot the dampness of the air, and felt the unending patter of the rain-drops on the barn roof merely a pleasant sort of accompaniment to the stories of their fancies.

Since the day when they had listened to Jones and Jerry joking, down below them in the barn, Rob had formed the habit of collecting every scrap of newspaper relating to the wonder. He cut paragraphs out of Aunt Matilda's cast-aside newspapers; he begged them from the farm-hands and from the country store-keepers. Anything in the form of an illustration he held as a treasure beyond price, and hoarded it to bring to Meg with exultant joy.

How they pored over these things, reading the paragraphs again and again, until they knew them almost by heart. How they studied the pictures, trying to gather the proportions and color of every column and dome and arch! What enthusiast, living in Chicago itself, knew the marvel as they did, and so dwelt on and revelled in its beauties! No one knew of their pleasure; like the Straw Parlor, it was their secret. The strangeness of their lives lay in the fact that absolutely no one knew anything about them at all, or asked anything, thinking it quite sufficient that their friendlessness was supplied with enough animal heat and nourishment to keep their bodies alive.

Of that other part of them—their restless, growing

young brains and naturally craving hearts, which in their own poor enough but still human little home had at least been recognized and cared for—Aunt Matilda knew nothing, and, indeed, had never given a thought to it. She had not undertaken the care of intelligences and affections; her own were not of an order to require supervision. She was too much occupied with her thousand-acre farm, and the amazing things she was doing with it. That the children could read and write and understood some arithmetic she knew. She had learned no more herself, and had found it enough to build her fortune upon. She had never known what it was to feel lonely and neglected, because she was a person quite free from affections and quite, enough for herself. She never suspected that others could suffer from a weakness of which she knew nothing, because it had never touched her.

If any one had told her that these two children, who ate her plentiful, rough meals at her table, among field-hands and servants, were neglected and lonely, and that their dim knowledge of it burned in their childish minds, she would have thought the announcement a piece of idle, sentimental folly; but that no solid detail of her farming was a fact more real than this one was the grievous truth.

"When we were at home," was Meg's summing-up of the situation, "at least we belonged to somebody. We were poor, and wore our clothes a long time, and had shabby shoes, and couldn't go on excursions, but we had

our little bench by the fire, and father and mother used to talk to us and let us read their books and papers, and try to teach us things. I don't know what we were going to be when we grew up, but we were going to do some sort of work, and know as much as father and mother did. I don't know whether that was a great deal or not, but it was something."

"It was enough to teach school," said Robin. "If we were not so far out in the country now, I believe Aunt Matilda would let us go to school if we asked her. It wouldn't cost her anything if we went to the public school."

"She wouldn't if we didn't ask her," said Meg. "She would never think of it herself. Do you know what I was thinking yesterday. I was looking at the pigs in their sty. Some of them were eating, and one was full, and was lying down going to sleep. And I said to myself, 'Robin and I are just like you. We live just like you. We eat our food and go to bed, and get up again and eat some more food. We don't learn anything more than you do, and we are not worth as much to anybody. We are not even worth killing at Christmas.'"

If they had never known any other life, or if nature had not given them the big, questioning eyes and square little jaws and strong, nervous little fists, they might have been content to sink into careless idleness and apathy. No one was actively unkind to them ; they had their Straw Parlor, and were free to amuse themselves as they chose. But they

had been made of the material of which the world's workers are built, and their young hearts were full of a restlessness and longing whose full significance they themselves did not comprehend.

And this wonder working in the world beyond them— this huge, beautiful marvel, planned by the human brain and carried out by mere human hands; this great thing with which all the world seemed to them to be throbbing, and which seemed to set no limit to itself and prove that there was no limit to the power of human wills and minds—this filled them with a passion of restlessness and yearning greater than they had ever known before.

"It is an enchanted thing, you know, Robin—it's an enchanted thing," Meg said one day, looking up from her study of some newspaper clippings and a magazine with some pictures in it.

"It seems like it," said Robin.

"I'm sure it's enchanted," Meg went on. "It seems so tremendous that people should think they could do such huge things. As if they felt as if they could do anything or bring anything from anywhere in the world. It almost frightens me sometimes, because it reminds me of the Tower of Babel. Don't you remember how the people got so proud that they thought they could do anything, and they began to build the tower that was to reach to heaven; and then they all woke up one morning and found they were all speaking different languages and could not understand each

other. Suppose everybody was suddenly struck like that some morning now—I mean the Fair people!" widening her eyes with a little shiver.

"They won't be," said Rob. "Those things have stopped happening."

"Yes, they have," said Meg. "Sometimes I wish they hadn't. If they hadn't, perhaps—perhaps if we made burnt offerings, we might be taken by a miracle to see the World's Fair."

"We haven't anything to burn," said Rob, rather gloomily.

"We've got the chickens," Meg answered as gloomily, "but it wouldn't do any good. Miracles are over."

"The world is all different," said Robin. "You have to do your miracle yourself."

"It will be a miracle," Meg said, "if we ever get away from Aunt Matilda's world, and live like people instead of like pigs who are comfortable—and we shall have to perform it ourselves."

"There is no one else," said Robin. "You see, there is no one else in the world."

He threw out his hand and it clutched Meg's, which was lying in the straw near him. He did not know why he clutched it—he did not in the least know why; nor did she know why a queer sound in his voice suddenly made her feel their unfriendedness in a way that overwhelmed her. She found herself looking at him, with a hard lump rising in her

throat.   It was one of the rainy days, and the hollow drum-
ming and patter of the big drops on the roof seemed somehow to shut them in with their loneliness away from all the
world.

"It's a strange thing," she said, almost under her breath,
"to be two children, only just twelve years old, and to be
quite by ourselves in such a big world, where there are such
millions and millions of people all busy doing things and
making great plans, and none of them knowing about us, or
caring what we are going to do."

"If we work our miracle ourselves," said Rob, holding
her hand quite tight, "it will be better than having it
worked for us.   Meg!"—as if he were beginning a new subject—"Meg!"

"What?" she answered, still feeling the hard lump in
her throat.

"Do you think we are going to stay here always?"

"I—oh, Robin, I don't know."

"Well, I do, then.   We are *not*—and that's the first step
up the Hill of Difficulty."

IV

ALL their lives the children had acted in unison. When they had been tiny creatures they had played the same games and used the same toys. It had seemed of little importance that their belongings were those of a boy and girl. When Robin had played with tops and marbles, Meg had played with them too. When Meg had been in a domestic and maternal mood, and had turned to dolls and dolls' housekeeping, Robin had assumed some masculine rôle connected with the amusement. It had entertained him as much at times to be the dolls' doctor, or the carpenter who repaired the dolls' furniture or made plans for the enlargement of the dolls' house, as it had entertained Meg to sew the flags and dress the sailors who manned his miniature ships, and assist him with the tails of his kites. They had had few playmates, and had pleased each other far better than outsiders could have done.

"It's because we are twins," Meg said. "Twins are made alike, and so they like the same things. I'm glad I'm a twin. If I had to be born again and be an *un*-twin I'm sure I should be lonely."

"I don't think it matters whether you are a boy or a

girl, if you are a twin," said Robin. " You are part of the other one, and so it's as if you were both."

They had never had secrets from each other. They had read the same books as they grew older, been thrilled by the same stories, and shared in each other's plans and imaginings or depressions. So it was a curious thing that at this special time, when they were drawn nearest to one another by an unusual interest and sympathy, there should have arrived a morning when each rose with a thought unshared by the other.

Aunt Matilda was very busy that day. She was always busy, but this morning seemed more actively occupied than usual. She never appeared to sit down, unless to dispose of a hurried meal or go over some accounts. She was a wonderful woman, and the twins knew that the most objectionable thing they could do was not to remove themselves after a repast was over; but this morning Meg walked over to a chair and firmly sat down in it, and watched her as she vigorously moved things about, rubbed dust off them, and put them in their right places.

Meg's eyes were fixed on her very steadily. She wondered if it was true that she and Robin were like her, and if they would be more like her when they had reached her age, and what would have happened to them before that time came. It was true that Aunt Matilda had a square jaw also. It was not an encouraging thing to contemplate; in fact, as she looked at her, Meg felt her heart begin a

"AUNT MATILDA," SHE SAID, SUDDENLY.

slow and steady thumping. But, as it thumped, she was getting herself in hand with such determination that when she at last spoke her chin looked very square indeed, and her black-lashed eyes were as nearly stern as a child's eyes can look.

"Aunt Matilda," she said, suddenly.

"Well?" and a tablecloth was whisked off and shaken.

"I want to talk to you."

"Talk in a hurry, then. I've no time to waste in talk."

"How old were you when you began to work and make money?"

Aunt Matilda smiled grimly.

"I worked out for my board when I was ten years old," she said. "Me and your father were left orphans, and we had to work, or starve. When I was twelve I got a place to wash dishes and look after children and run errands, and I got a dollar a week because it was out in the country, and girls wouldn't stay there."

"Do you know how old *I* am?" asked Meg.

"I've forgotten."

"I'm twelve years old." She got up from her chair and walked across the room, and stood looking up at Aunt Matilda. "I'm an orphan too, and so is Robin," she said, "and we have to work. You give us a place to stay in; but—there are other things. We have no one, and we have to do things ourselves; and we are twelve, and twelve is a good age for people who have to do things for

themselves. Is there anything in this house or in the dairy or on the farm that would be worth wages, that I could do? I don't care how hard it is if I can do it."

If Aunt Matilda had been a woman of sentiment she might have been moved by the odd, unchildish tenseness and sternness of the little figure, and the straight-gazing eyes, which looked up at her from under the thick black hair tumbling in short locks over the forehead. Twelve years old was very young to stand and stare the world in the face with such eyes. But she was not a woman of sentiment, and her life had been spent among people who knew their right to live could only be won by hard work, and who began the fight early. So she looked at the child without any emotion whatever.

"Do you suppose you could more than earn your bread if I put you in the dairy and let you help there?" she said.

"Yes," answered Meg, unflinchingly, "I know I could. I'm strong for my age, and I've watched them doing things there. I can wash pans and bowls and cloths, and carry things about, and go anywhere I'm told. I know how clean things have to be kept."

"Well," said Aunt Matilda, looking her over sharply, "they've been complaining about the work being too much for them, lately. You go in there this morning and see what you can do. You shall have a dollar a week if you're worth it. You're right about its being time that you should begin earning something."

"Thank you, ma'am," said Meg, and she turned round and walked away in the direction of the dairy, with two deep red spots on her cheeks and her heart thumping again—though this time it thumped quickly.

She reached the scene of action in the midst of a rush of work, and after their first rather exasperated surprise at so immature and inexperienced a creature being supposed to be able to help them, the women found plenty for her to do. She said so few words and looked so little afraid that she made a sort of impression on them.

"See," she said to the head woman, "Aunt Matilda didn't send me to do things that need teaching. Just tell me the little things, it does not matter what, and I'll do them. I can."

How she worked that morning—how she ran on errands—how she carried this and that—how she washed and scrubbed milk-pans—and how all her tasks were menial and apparently trivial, though entirely necessary, and how the activity and rapidity and unceasingness of them tried her unaccustomed young body, and finally made her limbs ache and her back feel as if it might break at some unexpected moment, Meg never forgot. But such was the desperation of her indomitable little spirit and the unconquerable will she had been born with, that when it was over she was no more in the mood for giving up than she had been when she walked in among the workers after her interview with Aunt Matilda.

When dinner-time came she walked up to Mrs. Macartney, the manager of the dairy work, and asked her a question.

"Have I helped you?" she said.

"Yes, you have," said the woman, who was by no means an ill-natured creature for a hard-driven woman. "You've done first-rate."

"Will you tell Aunt Matilda that?" said Meg.

"Yes," was the answer.

Meg was standing with her hands clasped tightly behind her back, and she looked at Mrs. Macartney very straight and hard from under her black brows.

"Mrs. Macartney," she said, "if I'm worth it, Aunt Matilda will give me a dollar a week; and it's time I began to work for my living. Am I worth that much?"

"Yes, you are," said Mrs. Macartney, "if you go on as you've begun."

"I shall go on as I've begun," said Meg. "Thank you, ma'am," and she walked back to the house.

After dinner she waited to speak to Aunt Matilda again.

"I went to the dairy," she said.

"I know you did," Aunt Matilda answered. "Mrs. Macartney told me about it. You can go on. I'll give you the dollar a week."

She looked the child over again, as she had done in the morning, but with a shade of expression which might have meant a touch of added interest. Perhaps her mind paused

just long enough to bring back to her the time when she had been a worker at twelve years old, and also had belonged to no one.

"She'll make her living," she said, as she watched Meg out of the room. "She's more like me than she is like her father. Robert wasn't worthless, but he had no push."

Having made quite sure that she was not wanted in the dairy for the time being, Meg made her way to the barn. She was glad to find it empty, so that she could climb the ladder without waiting. When she reached the top and clambered over the straw the scent of it seemed delightful to her. It was like something welcoming her home. She threw herself down full length in the Straw Parlor. Robin had not been at dinner. He had gone out early and had not returned. As she lay, stretching her tired limbs, and staring up at the nest in the dark, tent-like roof above her, she hoped he would come. And he did. In about ten minutes she heard the signal from the barn floor, and answered it. Robin came up the ladder rather slowly. When he made his way over the straw to her corner, and threw himself down beside her, she saw that he was tired too. They talked a few minutes about ordinary things, and then Meg thought she would tell him about the dairy. But it appeared that he had something to tell himself, and he began first.

"I've been making a plan, Meg," he said.

"Have you?" said Meg. "What is it?"

"I've been thinking about it for two or three days," he went on, "but I thought I wouldn't say anything about it until—till I tried how it would work."

Meg raised herself on her elbow and looked at him curiously. It seemed so queer that he should have had a plan too.

"Have you—tried?" she said.

"Yes," he answered, "I have been working for Jones this morning, and I did quite a lot. I worked hard. I wanted him to see what I could do. And then, Meg, I asked him if he would take me on—like the rest of the hands—and pay me what I was worth."

"And what did he say?" breathlessly.

"He looked at me a minute—all over—and half laughed, and I thought he was going to say I wasn't worth anything. It wouldn't have been true, but I thought he might, because I'm only twelve years old. It's pretty hard to be only twelve when you want to get work. But he didn't, he said, 'Well, I'm darned if I won't give you a show;' and I'm to have a dollar a week."

"Robin," Meg cried, with a little gasp of excitement, "so am I!"

"So are you!" cried Robin, and sat bolt upright. "*You!*"

"It's—it's because we are twins," said Meg, her eyes shining like lamps. "I told you twins did things alike because they couldn't help it. We have both thought of

the same thing. I went to Aunt Matilda, asked her to let me work somewhere and pay me, and she let me go into the dairy and try, and Mrs. Macartney said I was a help, and I am to have a dollar a week, if I go on as I've begun."

Robin's hand gave hers a clutch, just as it had done before, that day when he had not known why.

"Meg, I believe," he said, "I believe that we two will always go on as we begin. I believe we were born that way. We have to, we can't help it. And two dollars a week, if they keep us, and we save it all—we could go almost anywhere—sometime."

Meg's eyes were fixed on him with a searching, but half frightened, expression.

"Almost anywhere," she said, quite in a whisper. "Anywhere not more than a hundred miles away."

V

THEY did not tell each other of the strange and bold thought which had leaped up in their minds that day. Each felt an unwonted shyness about it, perhaps because it had been so bold; but it had been in each mind, and hidden though it was, it remained furtively in both.

They went on exactly as they had begun. Each morning Meg went to her drudgery in the dairy and Robin followed Jones whithersoever duty led. If the elder people had imagined they would get tired and give up they found out their mistake. That they were often tired was true, but that in either there arose once the thought of giving up, never! And they worked hard. The things they did to earn their weekly stipend would have touched the heart of a mother of cared-for children, but on Mrs. Jennings's model farm people knew how much work a human being could do when necessity drove. They were all driven by necessity, and it was nothing new to know that muscles ached and feet swelled and burned. In fact, they knew no one who did not suffer, as a rule, from these small inconveniences. And these children, with their set little faces and mature intelligence, were somehow so unsuggestive of the weakness and

limitations of childhood that they were often given work
which was usually intrusted only to elder people. Mrs.
Macartney found that Meg never slighted anything, never
failed in a task, and never forgot one, so she gave her
plenty to do. Scrubbing and scouring that others were
glad to shirk fell to her share. She lifted and dragged
things about that grown-up girls grumbled over. What
she lacked in muscle and size she made up in indomitable
will power that made her small face set itself and her small
body become rigid as iron. Her work ended by not con-
fining itself to the dairy, but extended to the house, the
kitchen—anywhere there were tiresome things to be done.

With Robin it was the same story. Jones was not afraid
to give him any order. He was of use in all quarters—in
the huge fields, in the barn, in the stables, and as a messenger to be trusted to trudge any distance when transport was
not available.

They both grew thin but sinewy looking, and their faces
had a rather strained look. Their always large black eyes
seemed to grow bigger, and their little square jaws looked
more square every day; but on Saturday nights they each
were paid their dollar, and climbed to the Straw Parlor and
unburied the Treasure and added to it.

Those Saturday nights were wonderful things. To the
end of life they would never forget them. Through all the
tired hours of labor they were looked forward to. Then
they lay in their nest of straw and talked things over—

there it seemed that they could relax and rest their limbs as they could do it nowhere else. Mrs. Jennings was not given to sofas and easy-chairs, and it is not safe to change position often when one has a grown-up bedfellow. But in the straw they could roll at full length, curl up or stretch out just as they pleased, and there they could enlarge upon the one subject that filled their minds, and fascinated and enraptured them.

Who could wonder that it was so! The City Beautiful was growing day by day, and the development of its glories was the one thing they heard talked of. Robin had established the habit of collecting every scrap of newspaper referring to it. He cut them out of Aunt Matilda's old papers, he begged them from every one, neighbors, store-keepers, work hands. When he was sent on errands he cast an all-embracing glance 'round every place his orders took him to. The postmaster of the nearest village discovered his weakness and saved paragraphs and whole papers for him. Before very long there was buried near the Treasure a treasure even more valuable of newspaper cuttings, and on the wonderful Saturday nights they gave themselves up to revelling in them.

How they watched it and followed it and lived with it— this great human scheme which somehow seemed to their young minds more like the scheme of giants and genii! How they seized upon every new story of its wonders and felt that there could be no limit to them! They knew

every purpose and plan connected with it—every arch and tower and hall and stone they pleased themselves by fancy-ing. Newspapers were liberal with information, people talked of it, they heard of it on every side. To them it seemed that the whole world must be thinking of nothing else.

"While we are lying here," Meg said—"while you are doing chores, and I am scouring pans and scrubbing things, it is all going on. People in France and in England and in Italy are doing work to send to it—artists are painting pict-ures, and machinery is whirring and making things, and everything is pouring into that one wonderful place. And men and women planned it, you know—just men and women. And if we live a few years we shall be men and women, and they were once children like us—only, if they had been quite like us they would never have known enough to do anything."

"But when they were children like us," said Robin, "they did not know what they would have learned by this time—and they never dreamed about this."

"That shows how wonderful men and women are," said Meg. "I believe they can do *anything* if they set their minds to it." And she said it stubbornly.

"Perhaps they can," said Robin, slowly. "Perhaps *we* could do anything we set our minds to."

There was the suggestive tone in his voice which Meg had been thrilled by more than once before. She had been

thrilled by it most strongly when he had said that if they saved their two dollars a week they might be able to go almost anywhere.   Unconsciously she responded to it now.

"If I could do anything I set my mind to," she said, "do you know what I would set my mind to first?"

"What?"

"I would set my mind to going to that wonderful place. I would set it to seeing everything there, and remembering all I could hold, and learning all there was to be learned— and I would *set it hard.*"

"So would I," said Robin.

It was a more suggestive voice than before that he said the words in; and suddenly he got up, and went and tore away the straw from the burying-place of the Treasure.   He took out the old iron bank, and brought it back to their corner.

He did it so suddenly, and with such a determined air, that Meg rather lost her breath.

"What are you going to do with the Treasure?" she asked.

"I am going to count it."

"Why?"

He was opening the box, using the blade of a stout pocket-knife as a screwdriver.

"A return ticket to Chicago costs fourteen dollars," he said.   "I asked at the dépôt.   That would be twenty-eight dollars for two people.   Any one who is careful can

live on a very little for a while. I want to see if we shall have money enough to *go*."

"To *go!*" Meg cried out. "To the Fair, Robin?"

She could not believe the evidence of her ears—it sounded so daring.

"Nobody would take us!" she said. "Even if we had money enough to pay for ourselves, nobody would take us."

"Take!" answered Robin, working at his screws. "No, nobody would. What's the matter with taking ourselves?"

Meg sat up in the straw, conscious of a sort of shock.

"To go by ourselves, like grown-up people! To buy our tickets ourselves, and get on the train, and go all the way—alone! And walk about the Fair alone, Robin?"

"Who takes care of us here?" answered Robin. "Who has looked after us ever since father and mother died? Ourselves! Just ourselves! Whose business are we but our own? Who thinks of us, or asks if we are happy or unhappy?"

"Nobody," said Meg. And she hid her face in her arms on her knees.

Robin went on stubbornly.

"Nobody is ever going to do it," he said, "if we live to be hundreds of years old. I've thought of it when I've been working in the fields with Jones, and I've thought of it when I've been lying awake at night. It's kept me awake many and many a time."

"So it has me," said Meg.

"And since this thing began to be talked about every-where, I've thought of it more and more," said Rob. "It means more to people like us than it does to any one else. It's the people who never see things, and who have no chances, it means the most to. And the more I think of it, the more I—I won't let it go by me!" And all at once he threw himself face downward on the straw, and hid his face in his arms.

Meg lifted hers. There was something in the woful desperation of his movement that struck her to the heart. She had never known him do such a thing in their lives before. That was not his way. Whatsoever hard thing had happened—howsoever lonely and desolate they had felt —he had never shown his feeling in this way. She put out her hand and touched his shoulder.

"Robin!" she said. "Oh, Robin!"

"I don't care," he said, from the refuge of his sleeves. "We *are* little when we are compared with grown-up people. They would call us children; and children usually have some one to help them and tell them what to do. I'm only like this because I've been thinking so much and working so hard—and it does seem like an Enchanted City —but no one ever thinks we could care about anything more than if we were cats and dogs. It was not like that at home, even if we were poor."

Then he sat up with as little warning as he had thrown

himself down, and gave his eyes a fierce rub.   He returned to the Treasure again.

"I've been making up my mind to it for days," he said. "If we have the money we can buy our tickets and go some night without saying anything to any one.   We can leave a note for Aunt Matilda, and tell her we are all right and we are coming back.   She'll be too busy to mind."

"Do you remember that book of father's we read?" said Meg.   "That one called 'David Copperfield.'   David ran away from the bottle place when he was younger than we are, and he had to walk all the way to Dover."

"We shall not have to walk; and we won't let any one take our money away from us," said Robin.

"Are we going, really?" said Meg.   "You speak as if we were truly going; and it *can't* be."

"Do you know what you said just now about believing human beings could do *anything*, if they set their minds to it?   Let's set our minds to it."

"Well," Meg answered, rather slowly, as if weighing the matter, "let's!"

And she fell to helping to count the Treasure.

VI

AFTERWARDS, when they looked back upon that day, they knew that the thing had decided itself then, though neither of them had said so.

"The truth was," Robin used to say, "we had both been thinking the same thing, as we always do, but we had been thinking it in the back part of our minds. We were afraid to let it come to the front at first, because it seemed such a big thing. But it went on thinking by itself. That time, when you said 'We shall *never* see it,' and I said, 'How do you know?' we were both thinking about it in one way; and I know I was thinking about it when I said, 'We are not going to stay here always. That is the first step up the Hill of Difficulty.'"

"And that day when you said you would not let it go by you," Meg would answer, "that was the day we reached the Wicket Gate."

It seemed very like it, for from that day their strange, unchildish purpose grew and ripened, and never for an hour was absent from the mind of either. If they had been like other children, living happy lives, full of young interests and pleasures, it might have been crossed out by other and

newer things; if they had been of a slighter mental build, and less strong, they might have forgotten it; but they never did. When they had counted the Treasure, and had realized how small it was after all, they had sat and gazed at each other for a while with grave eyes, but they had only been grave, and not despairing.

"Twenty-five dollars," said Robin. "Well, that's not much after nearly six years; but we saved it nearly all by cents, you know, Meg."

"And it takes a hundred cents to make a dollar," said Meg; "and we were poor people's children."

"And we bought the chickens," said Robin.

"And you have always given me a present at Christmas, Robin, even if it *was* only a little one. That's six Christmases."

"We have eight months to work in," said Robin, calculating. "If you get four dollars a month, and I get four, that will be sixty-four dollars by next June. Twenty-five dollars and sixty-four dollars make eighty-nine. Eighty-nine dollars for us to live on and go to see all the things; because we must see them all, if we go. And I suppose we shall have to come back"—with a long breath.

"Oh, dear!" cried Meg, "how *can* we come back?"

"I don't know," said Robin. "We shall hate it, but we have nowhere else to go."

"Perhaps we are going to seek our fortunes, and perhaps we shall find them," said Meg; "or perhaps Aunt

Matilda won't let us come back. Rob," with some awe, "do you think she will be angry?"

"I've thought about that," Robin answered contempla- tively, "and I don't think she will. She would be too busy to care much even if we ran away and said nothing. But I shall leave a letter, and tell her we have saved our money and gone somewhere for a holiday, and we're all right, and she need not bother."

"She won't bother even if she is angry," Meg said, with mournful eyes. "She doesn't care about us enough."

"If she loved us," Rob said, "and was too poor to take us herself, we couldn't go at all. We couldn't run away, because it would worry her so. You can't do a thing, how- ever much you want to do it, if it is going to hurt some- body who is good to you, and cares."

"Well, then, we needn't stay here because of Aunt Ma- tilda," said Meggy. "That's one sure thing. It wouldn't interfere with her ploughing if we were both to die at once."

"No," said Rob, deliberately, "that's just what it would *not.*" And he threw himself back on the straw and clasped his hands under his head, gazing up into the dark roof above him with very reflective eyes.

But they had reached the Wicket Gate, and from the hour they passed it there was no looking back. That in their utter friendlessness and loneliness they should take their twelve-year-old fates in their own strong little hands

was, perhaps, a pathetic thing ; that once having done so they moved towards their object as steadily as if they had been of the maturest years was remarkable, but no one ever knew or even suspected the first until the last.

The days went by, full of work, which left them little time to lie and talk in the Straw Parlor. They could only see each other in the leisure hours, which were so few, and only came when the day was waning. Finding them faithful and ready, those about them fell into the natural, easy, human unworthiness of imposing by no means infrequently on their inexperienced willingness and youth. So they were hard enough worked, but each felt that every day that passed brought them nearer to the end in view ; and there was always something to think of, some detail to be worked out mentally, or to be discussed, in the valuable moments when they were together.

"It's a great deal better than it used to be," Meg said, "at all events. It's better to feel tired by working than to be tired of doing nothing but think and think dreary things."

As the weather grew colder it was hard enough to keep warm in their hiding-place. They used to sit and talk, huddled close together, bundled in their heaviest clothing, and with the straw heaped close around them and over them.

There were so many things to be thought of and talked over ! Robin collected facts more sedulously than ever—

facts about entrance fees, facts about prices of things to eat, facts about places to sleep.

"Going to the Fair yourself, sonny?" Jones said to him one day. Jones was fond of his joke. "You're right to be inquirin' round. Them hotel-keepers is given to tot up bills several stories higher than their hotels is themselves."

"But I suppose a person needn't go to a hotel," said Robin. "There must be plenty of poor people who can't go to hotels, and they'll have to sleep somewhere."

"Ah, there's plenty of poor people," responded Jones, cheerfully, "plenty of 'em. Always is. But they won't go to Chicago while the Fair's on. They'll sleep at home—that's where they'll sleep."

"That's the worst of it," Rob said to Meg afterwards; "you see, we have to sleep *somewhere*. We could live on bread and milk or crackers and cheese—or oatmeal—but we have to *sleep* somewhere."

"It will be warm weather," Meg said, reflectively. "Perhaps we could sleep out of doors. Beggars do. We don't mind."

"I don't think the police would let us," Robin answered. "If they would—perhaps we might have to, some night; but we are going to that place, Meg—we are *going*."

Yes, they believed they were going, and lived on the belief. This being decided, howsoever difficult to attain, it was like them both that they should dwell upon the dream,

and revel in it in a way peculiarly their own. It was Meg whose imagination was the stronger, and it is true that it was always she who made pictures in words and told stories. But Robin was always as ready to enter into the spirit of her imaginings as she was to talk about them. There was a word he had once heard his father use which had caught his fancy, in fact, it had attracted them both, and they applied it to this favorite pleasure of theirs of romancing with everyday things. The word was "philander."

"Now we have finished adding up and making plans," he would say, putting his ten-cent account-book into his pocket, "let us philander about it."

And then Meg would begin to talk about the City Beautiful—a City Beautiful which was a wonderful and curious mixture of the enchanted one the whole world was pouring its treasures into, one hundred miles away, and that City Beautiful of her own which she had founded upon the one towards which Christian had toiled through the Slough of Despond and up the Hill of Difficulty and past Doubting Castle. Somehow one could scarcely tell where one ended and the others began, they were so much alike, these three cities—Christian's, Meg's, and the fair, ephemeral one the ending of the nineteenth century had built upon the blue lake's side.

"They must look alike," said Meg, "I am sure they must. See what it says in the 'Pilgrim's Progress.' 'Now just as the gates were opened to let in the men, I looked in

after them, and behold, the City shone like the sun'—and then it says, 'The talk they had with the Shining Ones was about the glory of the place; who told them that the beauty and glory of it were inexpressible.' I always think of it, Robin, when I read about those places like white palaces and temples and towers that are being built. I am so glad they are white. Think how the City will 'shine like the sun' when it stands under the blue sky and by the blue water, on a sunshiny day."

They had never read the dear old worn "Pilgrim's Progress" as they did in those days. They kept it in the straw near the Treasure, and always had it at hand to refer to. In it they seemed to find parallels for everything.

"Aunt Matilda's world is the City of Destruction," they would say. "And our loneliness and poorness are like Christian's 'burden.' We have to carry it like a heavy weight, and it holds us back."

"What was it that Goodwill said to Christian about it?" Robin asked.

Meg turned over the pages. She knew all the places by heart. It was easy enough to find and read how "At last there came a grave person to the gate, named Goodwill," and in the end he said, "As to thy burden, be content to bear it until thou comest to the place of deliverance; for there it will fall from thy back itself."

"But out of the 'Pilgrim's Progress,'" Robin said, with his reflecting air, "burdens don't fall off by themselves. If

you are content with them they stick on and get bigger. Ours would, I know. You have to do something yourself to get them off. But—" with a little pause for thought, "I like that part, Meg. And I like Goodwill, because he told it to him. It encouraged him, you know. You see it says next, 'Then Christian began to gird up his loins and address himself to his journey.'"

"Robin," said Meg, suddenly shutting the book and giving it a little thump on the back, "it's not only Christian's City that is like our City. *We* are like Christian. We are pilgrims, and our way to that place is our Pilgrims' Progress."

VII

AND the cold days of hard work kept going by, and the City Beautiful grew, and, huddled close together in the straw, the children planned and dreamed, and read and re-read the " Pilgrim's Progress," following Christian step by step.   And Aunt Matilda became busier every day, it seemed, and did not remember that they were alive except when she saw them.   And nobody guessed and nobody knew.

Days so quickly grow to weeks, and weeks slip by so easily until they are months, and at last there came a time when Meg, going out in the morning, felt a softer air, and stopped a moment by a bare tree to breathe it in and feel its lovely touch upon her cheek.   She turned her face upward with a half-involuntary movement, and found herself looking at such a limitless vault of tender blueness that her heart gave a quick throb, seemed to spring up to it, and carry her with it.   For a moment it seemed as if she had left the earth far below, and was soaring in the soft depths of blueness themselves.   And suddenly, even as she felt it, she heard on the topmost branch of the bare tree a brief little rapturous trill, and her heart gave a leap again, and she felt her cheeks grow warm.

"It is a bluebird," she said; "it is a bluebird. And it is the spring, and that means that the time is quite near."

She had a queer little smile on her face all day as she worked. She did not know it was there herself, but Mrs. Macartney saw it.

"What's pleasing you so, Meggy, my girl?" she asked.

Meg wakened up with a sort of start.

"I don't know—exactly," she said.

"You don't know," said the woman, good-naturedly. "You look as if you were thinking over a secret, and it was a pleasant one."

That evening it was not cold when they sat in the Straw Parlor, and Meg told Robin about the bluebird.

"It gave me a strange feeling to hear it," she said. "It seemed as if it was speaking to me. It said, 'You must get ready. It is quite near.'"

They had made up their minds that they would go in June, before the weather became so hot that they might suffer from it.

"Because we have to consider everything," was Robin's idea. "We shall be walking about all the time, and we have no cool clothes, and we shall have no money to buy cool things; and if we should be ill, it would be worse for us than for children who have some one with them."

In the little account-book they had calculated all they should own on the day their pilgrimage began. They had apportioned it all out: so much for the price of the railroad

tickets, so much for entrance fees, and—not so much, but so little—oh, so little!—for their food and lodging.

"I have listened when Jones and the others were talking," said Robin; "and they say that everybody who has room to spare, and wants to make money, is going to let every corner they have. So you see there will be sure to be people who have quite poor places that they would be obliged to rent cheap to people who are poor, like themselves. We will go through the small side streets and look."

The first bluebird came again, day after day, and others came with it, until the swift dart of blue wings through the air and the delicious ripple of joyous sound were no longer rare things. The days grew warmer, and the men threw off their coats, and began to draw their shirt-sleeves across their foreheads when they were at work.

One evening when Robin came up into the Straw Parlor he brought something with him. It was a battered old tin coffee-pot.

"What is that for?" asked Meg; for he seemed to carry it as if it was of some value.

"It's old and rusty, but there are no holes in it," Robin answered. "I saw it lying in a fence corner, where some one had thrown it—perhaps a tramp. And it put a new thought into my head. It will do to boil eggs in."

"Eggs!" said Meg.

"There's nothing much nicer than hard-boiled eggs," said Robin, "and you can carry them about with you. It

just came into my mind that we could take some of our eggs, and go somewhere where no one would be likely to see us, and build a fire of sticks, and boil some eggs, and carry them with us to eat."

"Robin," cried Meg, with admiring ecstasy, "I wish I had thought of that!"

"It doesn't matter which of us thought of it," said Rob, "it's all the same."

So it was decided that when the time came they should boil their supply of eggs very hard, and roll them up in pieces of paper and tuck them away carefully in the one small bag which was to carry all their necessary belongings. These belongings would be very few—just enough to keep them decent and clean, and a brush and comb between them. They used to lie in bed at night, with beating hearts, thinking it all over, sometimes awakening in a cold perspiration from a dreadful dream, in which Aunt Matilda or Jones or some of the hands had discovered their secret and confronted them with it in all its daring. They were so full of it night and day that Meg used to wonder that the people about them did not see it in their faces.

"They are not thinking of us," said Robin. "They are thinking about crops. I dare say Aunt Matilda would like to see the Agricultural Building, but she couldn't waste the time to go through the others."

Oh, what a day it was, what a thrilling, exciting, almost unbearably joyful day, when Robin gathered sticks and

dried bits of branches, and piled them in a corner of a field far enough from the house and outbuildings to be quite safe! He did it one noon hour, and as he passed Meg on his way back to his work, he whispered:

"I have got the sticks for the fire all ready."

And after supper they crept out to the place, with matches, and the battered old coffee-pot, and the eggs.

As they made their preparations, they found themselves talking in whispers, though there was not the least chance of any one's hearing them. Meg looked rather like a little witch as she stood over the bubbling old pot, with her strange, little dark face and shining eyes and black elf locks.

"It's like making a kind of sacrifice on an altar," she said.

"You always think queer things about everything, don't you?" said Robin. "But they're all right; I don't think of them myself, but I like them."

When the eggs were boiled hard enough they carried them to the barn and hid them in the Straw Parlor, near the Treasure. Then they sat and talked, in whispers still, almost trembling with joy.

"Somehow, do you know," Meg said, "it feels as if we were going to do something more than just go to the Fair. When people in stories go to seek their fortunes, I'm sure they feel like this. Does it give you a kind of creeping in your stomach whenever you think of it, Rob?"

MEG LOOKED RATHER LIKE A LITTLE WITCH.

"Yes, it does," Robin whispered back; "and when it comes into my mind suddenly something gives a queer jump inside me."

"That's your heart," said Meg. "Robin, if anything should stop us, I believe I should drop *dead*."

"No, you wouldn't," was Rob's answer, " but it's better not to let ourselves think about it. And I don't believe anything as bad as that *could* happen. We've worked so hard, and we have nobody but ourselves, and it can't do any one any harm—and we don't *want* to do any one any harm. No, there must be *something* that wouldn't let it be."

"I believe that too," said Meg, and this time it was she who clutched at Robin's hand; but he seemed glad she did, and held as close as she.

And then, after the bluebirds had sung a few times more, there came a night when Meg crept out of her cot after she was sure that the woman in the other bed was sleeping heavily enough. Every one went to bed early, and every one slept through the night in heavy, tired sleep. Too much work was done on the place to allow people to waste time in sleeplessness. Meg knew no one would waken as she crept down stairs to the lower part of the house and softly opened the back door.

Robin was standing outside, with the little leather satchel in his hand. It was a soft, warm night, and the dark blue sky was full of the glitter of stars.

Both he and Meg stood still a moment, and looked up.

"I'm glad it's like this," Meg said; "it doesn't seem so lonely.   Is your heart thumping, Robin?"

"Yes, rather," whispered Robin.   "I left the letter in a place where Aunt Matilda will be likely to find it some time to-morrow."

"What did you say?" Meg whispered back.

"What I told you I was going to.   There wasn't much to say.   Just told her we had saved our money, and gone away for a few days; and we were all right, and she needn't worry."

Everything was very still about them.   There was no moon, and, but for the stars, it would have been very dark. As it was, the stillness of night and sleep, and the sombreness of the hour, might have made less strong little creatures feel timid and alone.

"Let us take hold of each other's hands as we walk along," said Meg.   "It will make us feel nearer, and—and *twinner*."

And so, hand in hand, they went out on the road together.

VIII

IT was four miles to the dépôt, but they were good walkers. Robin hung the satchel on a stick over his shoulder; they kept in the middle of the road and walked smartly. There were not many trees, but there were a few, occasionally, and it was pleasanter to walk where the way before them was quite clear. And somehow they found themselves still talking in whispers, though there was certainly no one to overhear them.

"Let us talk about Christian," said Meg. "It will not seem so lonely if we are talking. I wish we could meet Evangelist."

"If we knew he was Evangelist when we met him," said Robin. "If we didn't know him, we should think he was some one who would stop us. And after all, you see, he only showed Christian the shining light, and told him to go to it. And we are farther on than that. We have passed the Wicket Gate."

"The thing we want," said Meg, "is the Roll to read as we go on, and find out what we are to do."

And then they talked of what was before them. They wondered who would be at the little dépôt and if they would

be noticed, and of what the ticket-agent would think when
Robin bought the tickets.

"Perhaps he won't notice me at all," said Rob. "And
he does not know me. Somebody might be sending us
alone, you know. We are not *little* children."

"That's true," responded Meg, courageously. "If we
were six years old it would be different. But we are
twelve!"

It did make it seem less lonely to be talking, and so they
did not stop. And there was so much to say.

"Robin," broke forth Meg once, giving his hand a sudden clutch, "we are on the way—we are *going*. Soon we
shall be in the train and it will be carrying us nearer
and nearer. Suppose it was a dream, and we should
wake up!"

"It isn't a dream!" said Rob, stoutly. "It's real—it's
as real as Aunt Matilda!" He was always more practical-
minded than Meg.

"We needn't philander any more," Meg said.

"It isn't philandering to talk about a real thing."

"Oh, Rob, just think of it—waiting for us under the
stars, this very moment—the City Beautiful!"

And then, walking close to each other in the dimness,
they told each other how they saw it in imagination, and
what its wonders would be to them, and which they would
see first, and how they would remember it all their lives
afterwards, and have things to talk of and think of. Very

few people would see it as they would, but they did not
know that. It was not a gigantic enterprise to them, a great
scheme fought for and struggled over for the divers reasons
poor humanity makes for itself ; that it would either make or
lose money was not a side of the question that reached
them. They only dwelt on the beauty and wonder of it,
which made it seem like an enchanted thing.

"I keep thinking of the white palaces, and that it is like
a fairy story," Meg said, "and that it will melt away like
those cities travellers sometimes see in the desert. And I
wish it wouldn't. But it will have been real for a while, and
everybody will remember it. I am so glad it is beautiful—
and white. I am *so* glad it is white, Robin !"

"And I keep thinking," said Robin, "of all the people
who have made the things to go in it, and how they have
worked and invented. There have been some people,
perhaps, who have worked months and months making one
single thing—just as we have worked to go to see it. And
perhaps, at first they were afraid they couldn't do it, and
they set their minds to it as we did, and tried and tried, and
then did it at last. I like to think of those men and women,
Meg, because, when the City has melted away, the things
won't melt. They will last after the people. And we are
people too. I'm a man, and you are a woman, you know,
though we are only twelve, and it gives me a strong feeling to think of those others."

"It makes you think that perhaps men and women *can*

do anything if they set their minds to it," said Meg, quite solemnly. "Oh, I do like that!"

"I like it better than anything else in the world," said Rob. "Stop a minute, Meg. Come here in the shade."

He said the last words quickly, and pulled her to the roadside, where a big tree grew which threw a deep shadow. He stood listening.

"It's wheels!" he whispered. "There is a buggy coming. We mustn't let any one see us."

It was a buggy, they could tell that by the lightness of the wheels, and it was coming rapidly. They could hear voices—men's voices—and they drew back and stood very close to each other.

"Do you think they have found out, and sent some one after us?" whispered Meg, breathlessly.

"No," answered Robin, though his heart beat like a triphammer. "No, no, no."

The wheels drew nearer, and they heard one of the men speaking.

"Chicago by sunrise," he was saying, "and what I don't see of it won't be worth seeing."

The next minute the fast-trotting horse spun swiftly down the road, and carried the voices out of hearing. Meg and Robin drew twin sighs of relief. Robin spoke first.

"It is some one who is going to the Fair," he said.

"Perhaps we shall see him in the train," said Meg.

"I dare say we shall," said Robin. "It was nobody who

knows us. I didn't know his voice. Meg, let's take hands again, and walk quickly ; we might lose the train."

They did not talk much more, but walked briskly. They had done a good day's work before they set out, and were rather tired, but they did not lag on that account. Sometimes Meg took a turn at carrying the satchel, so that Robin might rest his arm. It was not heavy, and she was as strong for a girl as he was for a boy.

At last they reached the dépôt. There were a number of people waiting on the platform to catch the train to Chicago, and there were several vehicles outside. They passed one which was a buggy, and Meg gave Robin a nudge with her elbow.

"Perhaps that belongs to our man," she said.

There were people enough before the office to give the ticket-agent plenty to do. Robin's heart quickened a little as he passed by with the group of maturer people, but no one seemed to observe him particularly, and he returned to Meg with the precious bits of pasteboard held very tight in his hand.

Meg had waited alone in an unlighted corner, and when she saw him coming she came forward to meet him.

"Have you got them ?" she said. "Did any one look at you or say anything ?"

"Yes, I got them," Robin answered. "And, I'll tell you what, Meg, these people are nearly all going just where we are going, and they are so busy thinking about it, and

attending to themselves, that they haven't any time to watch any one else.   That's one good thing."

"And the nearer we get to Chicago," Meg said, "the more people there will be, and the more they will have to think of.   And at that beautiful place, where there is so much to see, who will look at two children?   I don't believe we shall have any trouble at all."

It really did not seem likely that they would, but it happened, by a curious coincidence, that within a very few minutes they saw somebody looking at them.

The train was not due for ten minutes, and there were a few people who, being too restless to sit in the waiting-rooms, walked up and down on the platform.   Most of these were men, and there were two men who walked farther than the others did, and so neared the place where Robin and Meg stood in the shadow.   One was a young man, and seemed to be listening to instructions his companion, who was older, was giving him, in a rapid, abrupt sort of voice.   This companion, who might have been his employer, was a man of middle age.   He was robust of figure and had a clean-cut face, with a certain effect of strong good looks.   It was, perhaps, rather a hard face, but it was a face one would look at more than once; and he too, oddly enough, had a square jaw and straight black brows.   But it was his voice which first attracted Robin and Meg as he neared them, talking.

"It's the man in the buggy," whispered Robin.   "Don't

you know his voice again?" and they watched him with deep interest.

He passed them once, without seeming to see them at all. He was explaining something to his companion. The second time he drew near he chanced to look up, and his eye fell on them. It did not rest on them more than a second, and he went on speaking. The next time he neared their part of the platform he turned his glance towards them, as they stood close together. It was as if involuntarily he glanced to see if they were still where they had been before.

"A pair of children," they heard him say, as if the fleeting impression of their presence arrested his train of thought for a second. "Look as if no one was with them."

He merely made the comment in passing, and returned to his subject the next second; but Meg and Robin heard him, and drew farther back into the shadow.

But it was not necessary to stand there much longer. They heard a familiar sound in the distance, the shrill cry of the incoming train—the beloved giant who was to carry them to fairy-land; the people began to flock out of the waiting-rooms with packages and valises and umbrellas in hand; the porters suddenly became alert, and hurried about attending to their duties; the delightful roar drew nearer and louder, and began to shake the earth; it grew louder still, a bell began to make a cheerful tolling, people were

rushing to and fro; Meg and Robin rushed with them, and the train was panting in the dépôt.

It was even more thrilling than the children had thought it would be. They had travelled so very little, and did not know exactly where to go. It might not be the right train even. They did not know how long it would wait. It might rush away again before they could get on. People seemed in such a hurry and so excited. As they hurried along they found themselves being pushed and jostled. Before the steps of one of the cars a conductor stood, whom people kept showing tickets to. There were several persons round him when Robin and Meg reached the place where he stood. People kept asking him things, and sometimes he passed them on, and sometimes let them go into his car.

"Is this the train to Chicago?" said Robin, breathlessly.

But he was so much less than the other people, and the man was so busy, he did not hear him.

Robin tried to get nearer.

"Is this the Chicago train, sir?" he said, a little louder.

He had had to press by a man whom he had been too excited to see, and the man looked down, and spoke to him.

"Chicago train?" he said, in a voice which was abrupt, without being ill-natured. "Yes, you're all right. Got your sleeping tickets?"

"IS THIS THE TRAIN TO CHICAGO?" SAID ROBIN.

Robin looked up at him quickly. He knew the voice, and was vaguely glad to hear it. He and Meg had never been in a sleeping-car in their lives, and he did not quite understand. He held out his tickets.

"We are going to sleep on the train," he said; "but we have nothing but these."

"Next car but two, then," he said; "and you'd better hurry."

And when both voices thanked him at once, and the two caught each other's hands and ran towards their car, he looked after them and laughed.

"I'm blessed if they're not by themselves," he said, watching them as they scrambled up the steps. "And they're going to the Fair, I'll bet a dollar. *That's Young America*, and no mistake!"

IX

THE car was quite crowded. There were more people than themselves who were going to the Fair and were obliged to economize. When the children entered, and looked about them in the dim light, they thought at first that all the seats were full. People seemed to be huddled up asleep or sitting up awake in all of them. Everybody had been trying to get to sleep, at least, and the twins found themselves making their whispers even lower than before.

"I think there is a seat empty just behind that very fat lady," Meg whispered.

It was at the end of the car, and they went to it, and found she was right. They took possession of it quietly, putting their satchel under the seat.

"It seems so still," said Meg, "I feel as if I was in somebody's bedroom. The sound of the wheels makes it seem all the quieter. It's as if we were shut in by the noise."

"We mustn't talk," said Robin, "or we shall waken the people. Can you go to sleep, Meg?"

"I can if I can stop thinking," she answered, with a joyful sigh. "I'm very tired; but the wheels keep saying,

over and over again, 'We're going—we're going—we're going.' It's just as if they were talking. Don't you hear them?"

"Yes, I do. Do they say that to you, too? But we mustn't listen," Robin whispered back. "If we do we shall not go to sleep, and then we shall be too tired to walk about. Let's put our heads down, and shut our eyes, Meg."

"Well, let's," said Meg.

She curled herself up on the seat, and put her head into the corner.

"If you lean against me, Rob," she said, "it will be softer. We can take turns."

They changed position a little two or three times, but they were worn out with the day's work, and their walk, and the excitement, and the motion of the train seemed like a sort of rocking which lulled them. Gradually their muscles relaxed and they settled down, though, after they had done so, Meg spoke once, drowsily.

"Rob," she said, "did you see that was our man?"

"Yes," answered Rob, very sleepily indeed, "and he looked as if he knew us."

*   *   *   *   *

If they had been less young, or if they had been less tired, they might have found themselves awake a good many times during the night. But they were such children, and, now that the great step was taken, were so happy,

that the soft, deep sleepiness of youth descended upon and
overpowered them.   Once or twice during the night they
stirred, wakened for a dreamy, blissful moment by some
sound of a door shutting, or a conductor passing through.
But they were only conscious of a delicious sense of
strangeness, of the stillness of the car full of sleepers, of
the half-realized delight of feeling themselves carried along
through the unknown country, and of the rattle of the
wheels, which never ceased saying rhythmically, "We're
going—we're going—we're going!"

Ah! what a night of dreams and new, vague sensations,
to be remembered always!   Ah! that heavenly sense of joy
to come, and adventure, and young hopefulness and imagining!   Were there many others carried towards the City
Beautiful that night who bore with them the same rapture
of longing and belief; who saw with such innocent clear-
ness only the fair and splendid thought which had created
it, and were so innocently blind to any shadow of sordid-
ness or mere worldly interest touching its white walls?
And after the passing of this wonderful night, what a
wakening in the morning, at the first rosiness of dawn,
when all the other occupants of the car were still asleep, or
restlessly trying to be at ease!

It was as if they both wakened at almost the same
moment.   The first shaft of early sunlight streaming in the
window touched Meg's eyelids, and she slowly opened them.
Then something joyous and exultant rushed in upon her

heart, and she sat upright. And Robin sat up too, and they looked at each other.

"It's the Day, Meg!" said Robin. "It's the Day!" Meg caught her breath.

"And nothing has stopped us," she said. "And we are getting nearer and nearer. Rob, let us look out of the window."

For a while they looked out, pressed close together, and full of such ecstasy of delight in the strangeness of everything that at first they did not exchange even their whispers.

It is rather a good thing to see—rather well worth while even for a man or woman—the day waking, and waking the world, as one is borne swiftly through the morning light, and one looks out of a car window. What it was to these two children only those who remember the children who were themselves long ago can realize at all. The country went hurrying past them, making curious sudden revelations and giving half-hints in its haste; prairie and field, farmhouse and wood and village all wore a strange, exciting, vanishing aspect.

"It seems," Meg said, "as if it was all going somewhere—in a great hurry—as if it couldn't wait to let us see it."

"But we are the ones that are going," said Rob. "Listen to the wheels—and we shall soon be there."

After a while the people who were asleep began to stir

and stretch themselves.   Some of them looked cross, and
some looked tired.   The very fat lady in the seat before
them had a coal smut on her nose.

"Robin," said Meg, after looking at her seriously a
moment, "let's get our towel out of the bag and wet it and
wash our faces."

They had taken the liberty of borrowing a towel from
Aunt Matilda.   It was Meg who had thought of it, and it
had, indeed, been an inspiration.   Robin wetted two corners of it, and they made a rigorous if limited toilet.   At
least they had no smuts on their noses, and after a little
touching up with the mutual comb and brush, they looked
none the worse for wear.   Their plain and substantial gar-
ments were not of the order which has any special charm
to lose.

"And it's not our clothes that are going to the Fair,"
said Meg, "it's *us!*"

And by the time they were in good order, the farms and
villages they were flying past had grown nearer together.
The platforms at the dépôts were full of people who wore a
less provincial look; the houses grew larger and so did the
towns; they found themselves flashing past advertisements
of all sorts of things, and especially of things connected
with the Fair.

"You know how we used to play 'hunt the thimble,'"
said Robin, "and how, when any one came near the place
where it was hidden, we said, 'Warm—warmer—warmer

still—hot!' It's like that now. We have been getting warmer and warmer every minute, and now we are getting——"

"We shall be in in a minute," said a big man at the end of the car, and he stood up and began to take down his things.

"Hot," said Robin, with an excited little laugh. "Meg, we're not going—going—going any more. Look out of the window."

"We are steaming into the big dépôt," cried Meg. "How big it is! What crowds of people! Robin, we are there!"

Robin bent down to pick up their satchel; the people all rose in their seats and began to move in a mass down the aisle toward the door. Everybody seemed suddenly to become eager and in a hurry, as if they thought the train would begin to move again and carry them away. Some were expecting friends to meet them, some were anxious about finding accommodations. Those who knew each other talked, asked questions over people's shoulders, and there was a general anxiety about valises, parcels, and umbrellas. Robin and Meg were pressed back into their section by the crowd, against which they were too young to make headway.

"We shall have to wait until the grown-up people have passed by," Rob said.

But the crowd in the aisle soon lost its compactness,

and they were able to get out. The porter, who stood on the platform near the steps, looked at them curiously, and glanced behind them to see who was with them, but he said nothing.

It seemed to the two as if all the world must have poured itself into the big dépôt or be passing through it. People were rushing about; friends were searching for one another, pushing their way through the surging crowd; some were greeting each other with exclamations and hand-shaking, and stopping up the way; there was a Babel of voices, a clamor of shouts within the covered place, and from outside came a roar of sound rising from the city.

For a few moments Robin and Meg were overwhelmed. They did not quite know what to do; everybody pushed past and jostled them. No one was ill-natured, but no one had time to be polite. They were so young and so strange to all such worlds of excitement and rush, involuntarily they clutched each other's hands after their time-honored fashion, when they were near each other and overpowered. The human vortex caught them up and carried them along, not knowing where they were going.

"We seem so little!" gasped Meg. "There—there are so many people! Rob, Rob, where are we going?"

Robin had lost his breath too. Suddenly the world seemed so huge—so huge! Just for a moment he felt himself turn pale, and he looked at Meg and saw that she was pale too.

"Everybody is going out of the dépôt," he said. "Hold on to me tight, Meg. It will be all right. We shall get out."

And so they did. The crowd surged and swayed and struggled, and before long they saw that it was surging towards the entrance gate, and it took them with it. Just as they thrust through they found themselves pushed against a man, who good-naturedly drew a little back to save Meg from striking against his valise, which was a very substantial one. She looked up to thank him, and gave a little start. It was the man she had called "our man" the night before, when she spoke of him to Robin. And he gave them a sharp but friendly nod.

"Hallo!" he exclaimed, "it's you two again. You *are* going to the Fair!"

Robin looked up at his shrewd face with a civil little grin.

"Yes, sir; we are," he answered.

"Hope you'll enjoy it," said the man. "Big thing." And he was pushed past them and soon lost in the crowd.

X

THE crowd in the dépôt surged into the streets, and melted into and became an addition to the world of people there. The pavements were moving masses of human beings, the centres of the streets were pandemoniums of wagons and vans, street cars, hotel omnibuses, and carriages. The brilliant morning sunlight dazzled the children's eyes; the roar of wheels and the clamor of car bells, of clattering horses' feet, of cries and shouts and passing voices, mingled in a volume of sound that deafened them. The great tidal wave of human life and work and pleasure almost took them off their feet.

They knew too little of cities to have had beforehand any idea of what the overwhelming rush and roar would be, and what slight straws they would feel themselves upon the current. If they had been quite ordinary children, they might well have been frightened. But they were not ordinary children, little as they were aware of that important factor in their young lives. They were awed for this first moment, but, somehow, they were fascinated as much as they were awed, while they stood for a brief breathing-space looking on. They did not know—no child of their

ages can possibly know such things of him or herself—that Nature had made them of the metal out of which she moulds strong things and great ones. As they had not comprehended the restless sense of wrong and misery the careless, unlearning, and ungrowing life in Aunt Matilda's world filled them with, so they did not understand that, because they had been born creatures who belong to the great moving, working, venturing world, they were not afraid of it, and felt their first young face-to-face encounter with it a thing which thrilled them with an exultant emotion they could not have explained.

"This is not Aunt Matilda's world," said Rob. "It—I believe it is ours, Meg. Don't you?"

Meg was staring with entranced eyes at the passing multitude.

"'More pilgrims are come to town,'" she said, quoting the "Pilgrim's Progress" with a far-off look in her intense little black-browed face. "You remember what it said, Rob, 'Here also all the noise of them that walked in the streets was, More pilgrims are come to town.' Oh, isn't it like it!"

It was. And the exaltation and thrill of it got into their young blood and made them feel as if they walked on air, and that every passing human thing meant, somehow, life and strength to them.

Their appetites were sharpened by the morning air, and they consulted as to what their breakfast should be. They

had no money to spend at restaurants, and every penny must be weighed and calculated.

"Let's walk on," said Meg, "until we see a bakery that looks as if it was kept by poor people. Then we can buy some bread, and eat it with our eggs somewhere."

"All right," said Robin.

They marched boldly on. The crowd jostled them, and there was so much noise that they could hardly hear each other speak ; but ah ! how the sun shone, and how the pennons fluttered and streamed on every side, and how excited and full of living the people's faces looked ! It seemed splendid, only to be alive in such a world on such a morning. The sense of the practical which had suggested that they should go to a small place led them into the side streets. They passed all the big shops without a glance, but at last Meg stopped before a small one.

"There's a woman in there," she said; "I just saw her for a minute. She has a nice face. She looked as if she might be good-natured. Let's go in there, Robin. It's quite a small place."

They went in. It was a small place but a clean one, and the woman had a good-natured face. She was a German, and was broad and placid and comfortable. They bought some fresh rolls from her, and as she served them, and was making the change, Meg watched her anxiously. She was thinking that she did look very peaceable, indeed. So, instead of turning away from the counter,

she planted herself directly before her and asked her a question.

"If you please," she said, "we have some hard-boiled eggs to eat with our bread, and we are not going home. If we are very careful, would you mind if we ate our breakfast in here, instead of outside? We won't let any of the crumbs or shells drop on the floor."

"You not going home?" said the woman. "You from out town?"

"Yes," answered Meg.

"You look like you wass goun to der Fair," said the woman, with a good-tempered smile. "Who wass with you?"

"No one," said Robin. "We are going alone. But we're all right."

"My crayshious!" said the woman. "But you wass young for that. But your 'Merican childrens is queer ones. Yes! You can sit down an' eat your bregfast. That make no matter to me if you is careful. You can sit down."

There were two chairs near a little table, where, perhaps, occasional customers ate buns, and they sat down to their rolls and eggs and salt, as to a feast.

"I was hungry," said Rob, cracking his fourth egg.

"So was I!" said Meg, feeling that her fresh roll was very delicious.

It was a delightful breakfast. The German woman

watched them with placid curiosity as they ate it. She
had been a peasant in her own country, and had lived in a
village among rosy, stout, and bucolic little Peters and
Gretchens, who were not given to enterprise, and the
American child was a revelation to her. And somehow,
also, these two had an attraction all American children had
not. They looked so well able to take care of themselves,
and yet had such good manners and no air of self-impor-
tance at all. They ate their rolls and hard-boiled eggs
with all the gusto of very young appetite, but they evidently meant to keep their part of the bargain, and leave
her no crumbs and shells to sweep up. The truth was that
they were perfectly honorable little souls, and had a sense
of justice. They were in the midst of their breakfast,
when they were rather startled by hearing her voice from
the end of the counter where she had been standing, leaning against the wall, her arms folded.

"You like a cup coffee?" she asked.

They both looked round, uncertain what to say, not
knowing whether or not that she meant that she sold coffee.
They exchanged rather disturbed glances, and then Robin
answered.

"We can't afford it, thank you, ma'am," he said, "we've
got so little money."

"Never mind," she astonished them by answering, "that
cost me nothing. There some coffee left on the back of
the stove from my man's bregfast. I give you each a cup."

"YOU LIKE A CUP COFFEE?" SHE ASKED.

And she actually went into the little back room, and presently brought back two good cups of hot coffee.

"There, you drink that," she said, setting them down on the little table. "If you children goun to der Fair in that crowd by yourselves, you want something in your stomachs."

It was so good—it was so unexpected—it seemed such luck! They looked at each other with beaming eyes, and at her with quite disproportionate gratitude. It was much more than two cups of coffee to them.

"Oh, thank you," they both exclaimed. "We're so much obliged to you, ma'am!"

Their feast seemed to become quite a royal thing. They never had felt so splendidly fed in their lives. It seemed as if they had never tasted such coffee.

When the meal was finished, they rose refreshed enough to feel ready for anything. They went up to the counter and thanked the German woman again. It was Meg who spoke to her.

"We want to say thank you again," she said. "We are very much obliged to you for letting us eat our breakfast in here. It was so nice to sit down, and the coffee was so splendid. I dare say we do seem rather young to be by ourselves, but that makes us all the more thankful."

"That's all right," said the woman. "I hope you don't get lost by der Fair—and have good time!"

And then they went forth on their pilgrimage, into the

glorious morning, into the rushing world that seemed so splendid and so gay—into the fairy-land that only themselves and those like them could see.

"Isn't it nice when some one's kind to you, Rob?" Meg exclaimed joyfully, when they got into the sunshine. "Doesn't it make you feel happy, somehow, not because they've done something, but just because they've been kind?"

"Yes, it does," answered Rob, stepping out bravely. "And I'll tell you what I believe—I believe there are a lot of kind people in the world."

"So do I," said Meg. "I believe they're in it even when we don't see them."

And all the more, with springing steps and brave young faces, they walked on their way to fairy-land.

They had talked it all over—how they would enter their City Beautiful. It would be no light thing to them, their entrance into it. They were innocently epicurean about it, and wanted to see it at the very first in all its loveliness. They knew that there were gates of entrance here and there, through which thousands poured each day; but Meg had a fancy of her own, founded, of course, upon that other progress of the Pilgrim's.

"Robin," she said, "oh, we must go in by the water, just like those other pilgrims who came to town. You know that part at the last where it says, 'And so many went over the water and were let in at the golden gates

to-day.' Let us go over the water and be let in at the
golden gates. But the water we shall go over won't be
dark and bitter; it will be blue and splendid, and the sun
will be shining everywhere. Ah, Rob, how *can* it be true
that we are here!"

They knew all about the great arch of entrance and
stately peristyle. They had read in the newspapers all
about its height and the height of the statues adorning it;
they knew how many columns formed the peristyle, but it
was not height or breadth or depth or width they remembered. The picture which remained with them and haunted
them like a fair dream was of a white and splendid archway,
crowned with one of the great stories of the world in marble
—the triumph of the man in whom the god was so strong
that his dreams, the working of his mind, his strength, his
courage, his suffering, wrested from the silence of the Unknown a new and splendid world. It was this great white
arch they always thought of, with this precious marble story
crowning it, the blue, blue water spread before the stately
columns at its side, and the City Beautiful within the courts
it guarded. And it was to this they were going when they
found their way to the boat which would take them to it.

It was such a heavenly day of June! The water was so
amethystine, the sky such a vault of rapture! What did it
matter to them that they were jostled and crowded, and
counted for nothing among those about them? What did
it matter that there were often near them common faces,

speaking of nothing but common, stupid pleasure or common sharpness and greed? What did it matter that scarcely any one saw what they saw, or, seeing it, realized its splendid, hopeful meaning? Little recked they of anything but the entrancement of blue sky and water, and the City Beautiful they were drawing near to.

When first out of the blueness there rose the fair shadow of the whiteness, they sprang from their seats, and, hand in hand, made their way to the side, and there stood watching, as silent as if they did not dare to speak lest it should melt away; and from a fair white spirit it grew to a real thing—more white, more fair, more stately, and more an enchanted thing than even they had believed or hoped.

And the crowd surged about them, and women exclaimed and men talked, and there was a rushing to and fro, and the ringing of a bell, and movement and action and excitement were on every side. But somehow these two children stood hand in hand and only looked.

And their dream had come true, though it had been a child's dream of an enchanted thing.

XI

THEY passed beneath the snow-white stateliness of the
great arch, still hand in hand, and silent. They
walked softly, almost as if they felt themselves tread-
ing upon holy ground. To their youth and unworn souls it
was like holy ground, they had so dreamed of it, they had
so longed for it, it had been so mingled in their minds with
the story of a city not of this world.

And they stood within the court beyond the archway,
the fair and noble colonnade, its sweep of columns, statue-
crowned, behind them, the wonder of the City Beautiful
spread before. The water of blue lagoons lapped the bases
of white palaces, as if with a caress of homage to their
beauty. On every side these marvels stood ; everywhere
there was the green of sward and broad-leaved plants, the
sapphire of water, the flood of color and human life passing
by, and above it all and inclosing it, the warm, deep, splendid blueness of the summer sky.

It was so white—it was so full of the marvel of color—
it was so strange—it was so radiant and unearthly in its
beauty.

The two children only stood still and gazed and gazed,
with widening eyes and parted lips. They could not have

moved about at first; they only stood and lost themselves as in a dream.

Meg was still for so long that Robin, turning slowly to look at her at last, was rather awed.

"Meg!" he said; "Meg!"

"Yes," she answered, in a voice only half awake.

"Meg! Meg! We are *there!*"

"I know," said Meg. "Only it is so like—that other City—that it seems as if——" She gave a queer little laugh, and turned to look at him. "Rob," she said, "perhaps we are *dead*, and have just wakened up."

That brought them back to earth. They laughed together. No, they were not dead. They were breathless and uplifted by an ecstasy, but they had never been so fully *alive* before. It seemed as if they were in the centre of the world, and the world was such a bright and radiant and beautiful place as they had never dreamed of.

"Where shall we go first?" said Meg. "What shall we do?"

But it was so difficult to decide that. It did not seem possible to make a plan and follow it. It was not possible for them, at least. They were too happy and too young. Surely visitors to fairy-land could not make plans! They gave themselves up to the spell, and went where fancy led them. And it led them far, and through strange beauties, which seemed like dreams come true. They wandered down broad pathways, past green sward, waving palms,

glowing masses of flowers, white balustrades bordering lagoons lightly ruffled by a moment's wind. Wonderful statues stood on silent guard, sometimes in groups, sometimes majestic colossal figures.

"They look as if they were all watching the thousands and thousands go by," said Robin.

"It seems as if they must be thinking something about it all," Meg answered. "It could not be that they could stand there and look like that and not know."

It was she who soon after built up for them the only scheme they made during those enchanted days. It could scarcely be called a plan of action, it was so much an outcome of imagination and part of a vision, but it was a great joy to them through every hour of their pilgrimage.

Standing upon a fairy bridge, looking over shining canals crossed by these fairy bridges again and again, the gold sun lighting snow-white columns, archways, towers, and minarets, statues and rushing fountains, flowers and palms, her child eyes filled with a deep, strange glow of joy and dreaming.

She leaned upon the balustrade in her favorite fashion, her chin upon her hands.

"We need not *pretend* it is a fairy story, Robin," she said. "It *is* a fairy story, but it is real. Who ever thought a fairy story could come true? I've made up how it came to be like this."

"Tell us how," said Robin, looking over the jewelled water almost as she did.

"It was like this," she said.   "There was a great Magician who was the ruler of all the Genii in all the world. They were all powerful and rich and wonderful magicians, but he could make them obey him, and give him what they stored away.   And he said: 'I will build a splendid City, that all the world shall flock to and wonder at and remember forever.   And in it some of all the things in the world shall be seen, so that the people who see it shall learn what the world is like—how huge it is, and what wisdom it has in it, and what wonders! And it will make them know what *they* are like themselves, because the wonders will be made by hands and feet and brains just like their own. And so they will understand how strong they are—if they only knew it—and it will give them courage and fill them with thoughts.'"

She stopped a moment, and Rob pushed her gently with his elbow.

"Go on," he said, "I like it. It sounds quite true. What else?"

"And he called all the Genii together and called them by their names.   There was one who was the king of all the pictures and statues, and the people who worked at making them.   They did not know they had a Genius, but they had, and he put visions into their heads, and made them feel restless until they had worked them out into

statues and paintings. And the Great Genius said to him: 'You must build a palace for *your* people, and make them pour their finest work into it; and all the people who are made to be your workers, whether they know it or not, will look at your palace and see what other ones have done, and wonder if they cannot do it themselves.' And there was a huge, huge Genius who was made of steel and iron and gold and silver and wheels, and the Magician said to him: 'Build a great palace, and make your workers fill it with all the machines and marvels they have made, and all who see will know what wonders can be done, and feel that there is no wonder that isn't done that is too great for human beings to plan.' And there was a Genius of the strange countries, and one who knew all the plants and flowers and trees that grew, and one who lived at the bottom of the sea and knew the fishes by name and strode about among them. And each one was commanded to build a palace or to make his people work, and they grew so interested that in the end each one wanted his palace and his people to be the most wonderful of all. And so the City was built, and we are in it, Robin, though we are only twelve years old, and nobody cares about us."

"Yes," said Robin, "and the City is as much ours as if we were the Magician himself. Meg, who was the Magician? *What* was he?"

"I don't know," said Meg. "Nobody knows. He is that—that——" She gave a sudden, queer little touch to her

forehead and one to her side. "*That*, you know, Rob! The thing that *thinks*—and makes us want to do things and be things. Don't you suppose so, Rob?"

"The thing that made us want so to come here that we could not bear *not* to come?" said Robin. "The thing that makes you make up stories about everything, and always have queer thoughts?"

"Yes—that!" said Meg. "And every one has some of it; and there are such millions of people, and so there is enough to make the Great Magician. Robin, come along; let us go to the palace the picture Genius built, and see what his people put in it. Let us be part of the fairy story when we go anywhere. It will make it beautiful."

They took their fairy story with them and went their way. They made it as much the way of a fairy story as possible. They found a gondola with a rich-hued, gay-scarfed gondolier, and took their places.

"Now we are in Venice," Meg said, as they shot smoothly out upon the lagoon. "We can be in any country we like. Now we are in Venice."

Their gondola stopped, and lay rocking on the lagoon before the palace's broad white steps. They mounted them, and entered into a rich, glowing world, all unknown.

They knew little of pictures, they knew nothing of statuary, but they went from room to room, throbbing with enjoyment. They stopped before beautiful faces and

"NOW WE ARE IN VENICE."

happy scenes, and vaguely smiled, though they did not know they were smiling; they lingered before faces and figures that were sad, and their own dark little faces grew soft and grave. They could not afford to buy a catalogue, so they could only look and pity and delight or wonder.

"We must make up the stories and thoughts of them ourselves," Robin said. "Let's take it in turns, Meg. Yours will be the best ones, of course."

And this was what they did. As they passed from picture to picture, each took turns at building up explanations. Some of them might have been at once surprising and instructive to the artist concerned, but some were very vivid, and all were full of young directness and clear sight, and the fresh imagining and coloring of the unworn mind. They were so interested that it became like a sort of exciting game. They forgot all about the people around them; they did not know that their two small, unchaperoned figures attracted more glances than one. They were so accustomed to being alone, that they never exactly counted themselves in with other people. And now, it was as if they were at a banquet, feasting upon strange viands, and the new flavors were like wine to them. They went from side to side of the rooms, drawn sometimes by a glow of color, sometimes by a hinted story.

"We don't know anything about pictures, I suppose," said Meg, "but we can see everything is in them. There

are the poor, working in the fields and the mills, being glad or sorry; and there are the rich ones, dancing at balls and standing in splendid places."

"And there are the good ones and the bad ones. You can see it in their faces," Rob went on, for her.

"Yes," said Meg; "richness and poorness and goodness and badness and happiness and gladness. The Genius who made this palace was a very proud one, and he said he would put all the world in it, even if his workers could only make pictures and statues."

"Was he the strongest of all?" asked Robin, taking up the story again with interest.

"I don't know," Meg answered; "sometimes I think he was. He was strong—he was very strong."

They had been too deeply plunged into their mood to notice a man who stood near them, looking at a large picture. In fact, the man himself had not at first noticed them, but when Meg began to speak her voice attracted him. He turned his head, and looked at her odd little reflecting face, and, after having looked at it, he stood listening to her. An expression of recognition came into his strong, clean-shaven face.

"You two again!" he said, when she had finished. "And you have got here." It was their man again.

"Yes," answered Meg, her gray eyes revealing, as she lifted them to his face, that she came back to earth with some difficulty.

"How do you like it, as far as you've gone?" he asked.

"We are making believe that it is a fairy story," Meg answered; "and it's very easy."

And then a group of people came between and separated them.

XII

HOW tired they were when they came out from the world of pictures into the world of thronging people!

How their limbs ached and they were brought back to the realization that they were creatures with human bodies, which somehow they seemed to have forgotten!

When they stood in the sunshine again Robin drew a long breath.

"It is like coming out of one dream into another," he said. "We must have been there a long time. I didn't know I was tired and I didn't know I was hungry, but I am both. Are you?"

She was as tired and hungry as he was.

"Dare we buy a sandwich to eat with our eggs?" she said.

"Yes, I think we dare," Robin answered. "Where shall we go and eat them?"

There was no difficulty in deciding. She had planned it all out, and they so knew the place by heart that they did not need to ask their way. It was over one of the fairy bridges which led to a fairy island. It was softly wooded, and among the trees were winding paths and flowers and

rustic seats, and quaint roofs peering above the greenness of branches. And it was full of the warm scent of roses, growing together in sumptuous thousands, their heavy, sweet heads uplifted to the sun, or nodding and leaning towards their neighbors' clusters.

The fairy bridge linked it to the wonderful world beyond, but by comparison its bowers were almost quiet. The crowd did not jostle there.

"And we shall be eating our lunch near thousands and thousands of roses. It will be like the 'Arabian Nights.' Let us pretend that the rose who is queen of them all invited us, because we belong to nobody," Meg said.

They bought the modest addition to their meal, and carried the necessary, ever-present satchel to their bower. They were tired of dragging the satchel about, but they were afraid to lose sight of it.

"It's very well that it is such a small one, and that we have so little in it," Robin said. They chose the most secluded corner they could find, as near to the rose garden as possible, and sat down and fell upon their scant lunch as they had fallen upon their breakfast.

It was very scant for two ravenously hungry children, and they tried to make it last as long as possible. But scant as it was, and tired as they were, their spirits did not fail them.

"Perhaps, if we eat it slowly, it will seem more," said Meg, peeling an egg with deliberation, but with a very

undeliberate feeling in her small stomach. "Robin, did
you notice our man?"

"I saw him, of course," answered Robin; "he's too
big not to see."

"I *noticed* him," continued Meg. "Robin, there's something the matter with that man. He's a gloomy man."

"Well, you noticed him quickly," Robin responded,
with a shade of fraternal incredulity. "What's happened
to him?"

Meg's eyes fixed themselves on a glimpse of blue water
she saw through the trees. She looked as if she were
thinking the matter over.

"How do I know?" she said; "I couldn't. But, somehow, he has a dreary face, as if he had been thinking of
dreary things. I don't know why I thought that all in a
minute, but I did, and I believe it's true."

"Well, if we should see him again," Robin said, "I'll
look and see."

"I believe we shall see him again," said Meg. "How
many eggs have we left, Robin?"

"We only brought three dozen," he answered, looking
into the satchel; "and we ate seven this morning."

"When you have nothing but eggs, you eat a good
many," said Meg, reflectively. "They won't last very long.
But we couldn't have carried a thousand eggs, even if we
had had them"—which was a sage remark.

"We shall have to buy some cheap things," was Robin's

calculation. "They'll have to be very cheap, though. We have to pay a dollar, you know, every day, to come in ; and if we have no money we can't go into the places that are not free ; and we want to go into everything."

"I'd rather go in hungry than stay outside and have real dinners, wouldn't you?" Meg put it to him.

"Yes, I would," he answered, "though it's pretty hard to be hungry."

They had chosen a secluded corner to sit in, but it was not so secluded that they had it entirely to themselves. At a short distance from them, in the nearest bowery nook, a young man and woman were eating something out of a basket. They looked like a young country pair, plain and awkward, and enjoying themselves immensely. Their clothes were common and their faces were tanned, as if from working out of doors. But their basket evidently contained good, home-made things to eat. Meg caught glimpses of ham and chicken, and something that looked like cake. Just at that moment they looked so desperately good that she turned away her eyes, because she did not want to stare at them rudely. And as she averted them, she saw that Robin had seen, too.

"Those people have plenty to eat," he said, with a short, awkward laugh.

"Yes," she answered. "Don't let us look. We are *here*, Robin, anyway, and we knew we couldn't come as other people do."

"Yes," he said, "we are *here*."

The man and his wife finished their lunch, and began putting things in order in their basket. As they did it, they talked together in a low voice, and seemed to be discussing something. Somehow, in spite of her averted eyes, Meg suddenly felt as if they were discussing Robin and herself, and she wondered if they had caught her involuntary look.

"I think, Robin," said Meg—"I think that woman is going to speak to us."

It was evident that she was. She got up and came towards them, her husband following her rather awkwardly.

She stopped before them, and the two pairs of dark eyes lifted themselves to her face.

"I've just been talking to my man about you two," she said. "We couldn't help looking at you. Have you lost your friends?"

"No, ma'am," said Robin, "we haven't got any; I mean, we're not with any one."

The woman turned and looked at her husband.

"Well, Jem!" she exclaimed.

The man drew near and looked them over.

He was a raw-boned, big young man, with a countrified, good-natured face.

"You haven't come here alone?" he said.

"Yes," said Robin. "We couldn't have come, if we

"WELL, JEM!" SHE EXCLAIMED.

hadn't come alone. We're not afraid, thank you. We're getting along very well."

"Well, Jem!" said the woman again.

She seemed quite stirred. There was something in her ordinary, good-natured face that was quite like a sort of rough emotion.

"Have you plenty of money?" she asked.

"No," said Robin, "not plenty, but we have a little."

She put her basket down and opened it. She took out some pieces of brown fried chicken; then she took out some big slices of cake, with raisins in it. She even added some biscuits and slices of ham. Then she put them in a coarse, clean napkin.

"Now, look here," she said, "don't you go filling up with candy and peanuts, just because you are by yourselves. You put this in your bag, and eat it when you're ready. 'T any rate, it's good, home-made victuals, and won't harm you."

And in the midst of their shy thanks, she shut the basket again and went off with her husband, and they heard her say again, before she disappeared,

"Well, Jem!"

XIII

YES, there were plenty of kind people in the world, and one of the best proofs of it was that, in that busy, wonderful place through which all the world seemed passing, and where, on every side, were a thousand things to attract attention, and so fill eyes and mind that forgetfulness and carelessness of small things might not have been quite unnatural, these two small things, utterly insignificant and unknown to the crowds they threaded, met many a passing friend of the moment, and found themselves made happier by many a kindly and helpful word or look. Officials were good-natured to them, guides were good-humored, motherly women and fatherly men protected them in awkward crowds. They always saw that those who noticed them glanced about for their chaperons, and again and again they were asked who was taking care of them; but Robin's straightforward, civil little answer, "We're taking care of ourselves," never failed to waken as much friendly interest as surprise.

They kept up their fairy story of the Great Genius, and called things by fairy-story names, and talked to each other of their fairy-story fancies about them. It was so

much more delightful to say: "Let us go to the Palace of the Genius of the Sea," than to say, "Let us go to the Fisheries' building." And once in the palace, standing among great rocks and pools and fountains, with water splashing and tumbling over strange sea-plants, and strange sea-monsters swimming beneath their eyes in green sea-water, it was easy to believe in the Genius who had brought them all together.

"He was very huge," Meg said, making a picture of him. "He had monstrous eyes, that looked like the sea when it is blue; he had great, white coral teeth, and he had silver, scaly fish-skin wound round him, and his hair was long sea-grass and green and brown weeds."

They stood in grottoes and looked down into clear pools, at swift-darting things of gold and silver and strange prismatic colors. Meg made up stories of tropical rivers, with palms and jungle cane fringing them, and tigers and lions coming to lap at the brink. She invented rushing mountain streams and lakes, with speckled trout leaping; and deep, deep seas, where whales lay rocking far below, and porpoises rolled, and devil-fish spread hideous, far-reaching tentacles for prey.

Oh, what a day it was! What wonders they saw and hung over, and dwelt on with passions of young delight! The great sea gave up its deep to them; great forests and trackless jungles their wonderful growths; kings' palaces and queens' coffers their rarest treasures; the ages of long

ago their relics and strange legends, in stone and wood and brass and gold.

They did not know how often people turned and stopped to look at their two little, close-leaning figures and vivid, dark, ecstatic-eyed faces. They certainly never chanced to see that one figure was often behind them at a safe distance, and seemed rather to have fallen into the habit of going where they went and listening to what they said. It was their man, curiously enough, and it was true that he was rather a gloomy-looking man, when one observed him well. His keen, business-like, well-cut face had a cloud resting upon it ; he looked listless and unsmiling, even in the palaces that most stirred the children's souls ; and, in fact, it seemed to be their odd enthusiasm which had attracted him a little, because he was in the mood to feel none himself. He had been within hearing distance when Meg had been telling her stories of the Genius of the Palace of the Sea, and a faint smile had played about his mouth for a moment. Then he had drawn a trifle nearer, still keeping out of sight, and when they had moved he had followed them. He had been a hard, ambitious, wealth-gaining man all his life. A few years before he had found a new happiness, which softened him for a while, and made his world seem a brighter thing. Then a black sorrow had come upon him, and everything had changed. He had come to the Enchanted City, not as the children had come, because it shone before them, a radiant joy, but because he wondered if it would distract

HE WAS LOOKING AT HER IN AN ABSENT, MISERABLE WAY.

him at all. All other things had failed ; his old habits of work and scheme, his successes, his ever-growing fortune, they were all as nothing. The world was empty to him, and he walked about it feeling like a ghost. The little dark, vivid faces had attracted him, he did not know why, and when he heard the story of the Palace of the Sea he was led on by a vague interest.

He was near them often during the day, but it was not until late in the afternoon that they saw him themselves, when he did not see them. They came upon him in a quiet spot where he was sitting alone. On a seat near him sat a young woman, resting, with a baby asleep in her arms. The young woman was absorbed in her child, and was apparently unconscious of him. His arms were folded and his head bent, but he was looking at her in an absent, miserable way. It was as if she made him think of something bitter and sad.

Meg and Robin passed him quietly.

" I see what you meant, Meg," Robin said. " He does look as if something was the matter with him. I wonder what it is ? "

When they passed out of the gates at dusk, it was with worn-out bodies, but enraptured souls. In the street-car, which they indulged in the extravagance of taking, the tired people, sitting exhaustedly in the seats and hanging on to straps, looked with a sort of wonder at them, their faces shone so like stars. They did not know where they

were going to sleep, and they were more than ready for lying down, but they were happy beyond words.

They went with the car until it reached the city's heart, and then they got out and walked. The streets were lighted, and the thoroughfares were a riot of life and sound. People were going to theatres, restaurants, and hotels, which were a blaze of electric radiance. They found themselves limping a little, but they kept stoutly on, holding firmly to the satchel.

"We needn't be afraid of going anywhere, however poor it looks," Robin said, with a grave little elderly air. He was curiously grave for his years, sometimes. "Anybody can see we have nothing to steal. I think any one would know that we only want to go to bed."

It was a queer place they finally hit upon. It was up a side street, which was poorly lighted, and where the houses were all shabby and small. On the steps of one of them a tired-looking woman was sitting, with a pale, old-faced boy beside her. Robin stopped before her.

"Have you a room where my sister could sleep, and I could have a mattress on the floor, or lie down on anything?" he said. "We can't afford to go anywhere where it will cost more than fifty cents each."

The woman looked at them indifferently. She was evidently very much worn out with her day's work, and discouraged by things generally.

"I haven't anything worth more than fifty cents, good-

ness knows," she answered. "You must be short of money to come here. I've never thought of having roomers."

"We're poor," said Robin, "and we know we can't have anything but a poor room. If we can lie down, we are so tired we shall go to sleep anywhere. We've been at the Fair all day."

The pale little old-faced boy leaned forward, resting his arm on his mother's knee. They saw that he was a very poor little fellow, indeed, with a hunch back.

"Mother," he said, "let 'em stay; I'll sleep on the floor."

The woman gave a dreary half laugh, and got up from the step. "He's crazy about the Fair," she said. "We hain't no money to spend on Fairs, and he's most wild about it. You can stay here to-night, if you want to."

She made a sign to them to follow her. The hunchback boy rose too, and went into the dark passage after them. He seemed to regard them with a kind of hunger in his look.

They went up the narrow, steep staircase. It was only lighted by a dim gleam from a room below, whose door was open. The balustrades were rickety, and some of them were broken out. It was a forlorn enough place. The hunchback boy came up the steps, awkwardly, behind them. It was as if he wanted to see what would happen.

They went up two flights of the crooked, crazy stairs, and at the top of the second flight the woman opened a door.

"That's all the place there is," she said. "It isn't any-thing more than a place to lie down in, you see. I can put a mattress on the floor for you, and your sister can sleep in the cot."

"That's all we want," replied Robin.

But it was a poor place. A room, both small and bare, and with broken windows. There was nothing in it but the cot and a chair.

"Ben sleeps here," the woman said. "If I couldn't make him a place on the floor, near me, I couldn't let it to you." Meg turned and looked at Ben. He was gazing at her with a nervous interest.

"We're much obliged to you," she said.

"It's all right," he said, with eager shyness. "Do you want some water to wash yourselves with? I can bring you up a tin basin and a jug. You can set it on the chair."

"Thank you," they both said at once. And Robin added, "We want washing pretty badly."

Ben turned about and went down-stairs for the water as if he felt a sort of excitement in doing the service. These two children, who looked as poor as himself, set stirring strange thoughts in his small, unnourished brain.

He brought back the tin basin and water, a piece of yellow soap, and even a coarse, rather dingy, towel. He had been so eager that he was out of breath when he returned, but he put the basin on the chair and the tin

jug beside it, with a sort of exultant look in his poor face.

"Thank you," said Meg again; "thank you, Ben."

She could not help watching him as his mother prepared the rather wretched mattress for Robin. Once he caught the look of her big, childish, gray eyes as it rested upon him with questioning sympathy, and he flushed up so that even by the light of the little smoky lamp she saw it. When the woman had finished she and the boy went away and left them, and they stood a moment looking at each other. They were both thinking of the same thing, but somehow they did not put it into words.

"We'll wash off the dust first," said Robin, "and then we'll eat some of the things we have left from what the woman gave us. And then we'll go to bed, and we shall drop just like logs."

And this they did, and it was certainly a very short time before the smoky little lamp was out, and each had dropped like a log and lay stretched in the darkness, with a sense of actual ecstasy in limbs laid down to rest and muscles relaxed for sleeping.

"Robin," said Meg, drowsily, through the dark that divided them, "everybody in the world has something to give to somebody else."

"I'm thinking that, too," Robin answered, just as sleepily; "nobody is so poor—that—he—hasn't anything. That —boy——"

"He let us have his hard bed," Meg murmured, "and he
—hasn't seen——"

But her voice died away, and Robin would not have
heard her if she had said more.   And they were both fast,
fast asleep.

XIV

IT would have been a loud sound which would have awakened them during those deep sleeping hours of the night. They did not even stir on their poor pillows when, long after midnight, there was the noise of heavy drunken footsteps and heavy drunken stumbling in the passage below, and then the raising of a man's rough voice, and the upsetting of chairs and the slamming of doors, mingled with the expostulations of the woman, whose husband had come home in something worse than his frequent ill-fashion. They slept sweetly through it all, but when the morning came, and hours of unbroken rest had made their slumbers lighter, and the sunshine streamed in through the broken windows, they were called back to the world by loud and angry sounds.

"What is it?" said Meg, sitting bolt upright and rubbing her eyes; "somebody's shouting."

"And somebody's crying," said Robin, sitting up too, but more slowly.

It was quite clear to them, as soon as they were fully awake, that both these things were happening. A man seemed to be quarrelling below. They could hear him stamping about and swearing savagely. And they could

hear the woman's voice, which sounded as if she were trying
to persuade him to do or leave undone something.   They
could not hear her words, but she was crying, and somebody
else was crying, too, and they knew it was the boy with the
little old face and the hump back.

"I suppose it's the woman's husband," said Meg.   "I'm
glad he wasn't here last night."

"I wonder if he knows we are here," said Robin, listening anxiously.

It was plain that he did know.   They heard him
stumbling up the staircase, grumbling and swearing as he
came, and he was coming up to their room, it was evident.

"What shall we do?" exclaimed Meg, in a whisper.

"Wait," Robin answered, breathlessly.   "We can't do
anything."

The heavy feet blundered up the short second flight and
blundered to their door.   It seemed that the man had not
slept off his drunken fit.   He struck the door with his fist.

"Hand out that dollar," he shouted.   "When my wife
takes roomers I'm going to be paid.   Hand it out."

They heard the woman hurrying up the stairs after him.
She was out of breath with crying, and there was a chok-
ing sound in her voice when she spoke to them through
the door.

"You'd better let him have it," she said.

"I guess they'd better," said the man, roughly.   "Who
d' they suppose owns the house?"

Robin got up and took a dollar from their very small store, which was hidden in the lining of his trousers. He went to the door and opened it a little, and held the money out.

" Here it is," he said.

The man snatched it out of his hand and turned away, and went stumbling down stairs, still growling. The woman stood a minute on the landing, and they heard her make a pitiful sort of sound, half sob, half sniff.

Meg sat up in bed, with her chin on her hands, and glared like a little lioness.

" What do you think of *that?* " she said.

" He's a devil!" said Robin, with terseness. And he was conscious of no impropriety. " I wanted that boy to have it, and *go*." It was not necessary to say where.

" So did I," answered Meg. " And I believe his mother would have given it to him, too."

They heard the man leave the house a few minutes later, and then it did not take them long to dress and go down the narrow, broken-balustraded stairs again. As they descended the first flight they saw the woman cooking something over the stove in her kitchen, and as she moved about they saw her brush her apron across her eyes.

The squalid street was golden with the early morning sunshine, which is such a joyful thing, and, in the full, happy flood of it, a miserable little figure sat crouched on the steps. It was the boy Ben, and they saw that he

looked paler than he had looked the night before, and his little face looked older. His elbow was on his knee and his cheek on his hand, and there were wet marks on his cheeks.

A large lump rose up in Meg's throat.

" I know what's the matter," she whispered to Robin.

" So—so do I," Robin answered, rather unsteadily. " And he's poorer than anybody else. It *ought* not to go by him."

" No, no, " said Meg. " It oughtn't."

She walked straight to the threshold and sat down on the step beside him. She was a straightforward child, and she was too much moved to stand on ceremony. She sat down quite close by the poor little fellow, and put her hand on his arm.

" Never you mind," she said. " Never you mind." And her throat felt so full that for a few seconds she could say nothing more.

Robin stood against the door post. The effect of this was to make his small jaw square itself.

" Don't mind us at all," he said. " We—we know."

The little fellow looked at Meg and then up at him. In that look he saw that they did know.

" Mother was going to give that dollar to me," he said, brokenly. " I was going to the Fair on it. *Everybody* is going, everybody is talking about it, and thinking about it ! Nobody's been talking of nothing else for months and

months! The streets are full of people on their way! And they all pass me by."

He rubbed his sleeve across his forlorn face and swallowed hard.

"There's pictures in the shops," he went on, "and flags flying. And everything's going that way, and me staying behind!"

Two of the large, splendid drops, which had sometimes gathered on Meg's eyelashes and fallen on the straw, when she had been telling stories in the barn, fell now upon her lap.

"Robin!" she said.

Robin stood and stared very straight before him for a minute, and then his eyes turned and met hers.

"We're very poor," he said to her, "but *everybody* has —has something."

"We couldn't leave him behind," Meg said, "we *couldn't!* Let's think." And she put her head down, resting her elbows on her knee and clutching her forehead with her supple, strong little hands.

"What can we do without?" said Robin. "Let's do without something."

Meg lifted her head.

"We will eat nothing but the eggs for breakfast," she said, "and go without lunch—if we can. Perhaps we can't —but we'll try. And we will not go into some of the places we have to pay to go into. I will make up stories about

them for you.   And, Robin, it *is* true—everybody has something to give.   That's what I have—the stories I make up.
It's *something*—just a little."

"It isn't so little," Robin answered ; "it fills in the empty
place, Meg ?" with a question in his voice.

She answered with a little nod, and then put her hand on
Ben's arm again.   During their rapid interchange of words
he had been gazing at them in a dazed, uncomprehending
way.   To his poor little starved nature they seemed so
strong and different from himself that there was something
wonderful about them.   Meg's glowing, dark little face
quite made his weak heart beat as she turned it upon him.

"We are not much better off than you are," she said,
"but we think we've got enough to take you into the
grounds.   You let us have your bed.   Come along with us."

"To—to—the Fair ?" he said, tremulously.

"Yes," she answered, "and when we get in I'll try and
think up things to tell you and Robin, about the places we
can't afford to go into.   We can go into the Palaces for
nothing."

"Palaces !" he gasped, his wide eyes on her face.
She laughed.

"That's what we call them," she said ; "that's what they
are.   It's part of a story.   I'll tell it to you as we go."

"Oh !" he breathed out, with a sort of gasp, again.

He evidently did not know how to express himself.   His
hands trembled, and he looked half frightened.

"TO—TO—THE FAIR?" HE SAID, TREMULOUSLY.

"If you'll do it," he said, "I'll remember you all my life! I'll—I'll—if it wasn't for father I know mother would let you sleep here every night for nothing. And I'd give you my bed and be glad to do it, I would. I'll be so thankful to you. I hain't got nothin'—nothin'—but I'll be that thankful —I"—there was a kind of hysterical break in his voice— "let me go and tell mother," he said, and he got up stumblingly and rushed into the house.

Meg and Robin followed him to the kitchen, as excited as he was. The woman had just put a cracked bowl of something hot on the table, and as he came in she spoke to him.

"Your mush is ready," she said. "Come and eat while it's hot."

"Mother," he cried out, "they are going to take me in. I'm going! They're going to take me!"

The woman stopped short and looked at the twins, who stood in the doorway. It seemed as if her chin rather trembled.

"You're going—" she began, and broke off. "You're as poor as he is," she ended. "You must be, or you wouldn't have come here to room."

"We're as poor in one way," said Meg, "but we worked, and saved money to come. It isn't much, but we can do without something that would cost fifty cents, and that will pay for his ticket."

The woman's chin trembled more still.

"Well," she said, "I—I—O Lord!" And she threw her apron over her head and sat down suddenly.

Meg went over to her, not exactly knowing why.

"We could not bear to go ourselves," she said. "And he is like us."

She was thinking, as she spoke, that this woman and her boy were very fond of each other. The hands holding the apron were trembling as his had done. They dropped as suddenly as they had been thrown up. The woman lifted her face eagerly.

"What were you thinking of going without?" she asked. "Was it things to eat?"

"We—we've got some hard-boiled eggs," faltered Meg, a little guiltily.

"There's hot mush in the pan," said the woman. "There's nothing to eat with it, but it's healthier than cold eggs. Sit down and eat some."

And they did, and in half an hour they left the poor house, feeling full-fed and fresh. With them went Ben—his mother standing on the steps looking after him—his pale old face almost flushed and young, as it set itself toward the City Beautiful.

XV

BEFORE they entered the Court of Honor Meg stopped them both. She was palpitating with excitement.

"Robin," she said, "let us make him shut his eyes. Then you can take one of his hands and I can take the other, and we will lead him. And when we have taken him to the most heavenly place, he shall look—suddenly!"

"I should like that," said Ben, tremulous with anticipation.

"All right," said Robin.

By this time it was as if they had been friends all their lives. They knew each other. They had not ceased talking a moment since they set out, but it had not been about the Fair. Meg had decided that nothing should be described beforehand; that all the entrancement of beauty should burst upon Ben's hungry soul, as Paradise bursts upon translated spirits.

"I don't want it to be gradual," she said, anxiously. "I want it to be *sudden!* It can be gradual after."

She was an artist and an epicure in embryo, this child. She tasted her joys with a delicate palate, and lost no flavor of them. The rapture of yesterday was intensified

tenfold to-day, because she felt it throbbing anew in this frail body beside her, in which Nature had imprisoned a soul as full of longings as her own, but not so full of power.

They took Ben by either hand, and led him with the greatest care. He shut his eyes tight, and walked between them. People who glanced at them smiled, recognizing the time-honored and familiar child trick. They did not know that this time it was something more than that.

"The trouble is," Meg said in a low voice to Robin, "I don't know which is the most heavenly place to stand. Sometimes I think it is at one end, and sometimes at the other, and sometimes at the side."

They led their charge for some minutes indefinitely. Sometimes they paused and looked about them, speaking in undertones. Ben was rigidly faithful, and kept his eyes shut. As they hesitated for a moment near one of the buildings, a man who was descending the steps looked in their direction, and his look was one of recognition. It was the man who had watched them the day before, and he paused upon the steps, interested again, and conscious of being curious.

"What are they going to do?" he said to himself. "They are going to do something. Where did they pick up the other one—poor little chap!"

Meg had been looking very thoughtful during that moment of hesitancy. She spoke, and he was near enough to hear her.

"He shall open them where he can hear the water splashing in the fountain," she said. "I think that's the best."

It seemed that Robin thought so, too. They turned and took their way to the end of the Court, where the dome lifted itself, wonderful, against the sky, and a splendor of rushing water, from which magnificent sea-monsters rose, stood grand before.

Their man followed them. He had had a bad night, and had come out into a dark world. The streams of pleasure-seekers, the gayly fluttering flags, the exhilaration in the very air seemed to make his world blacker and more empty. A year before he had planned to see this wonder, with the one soul on earth who would have been most thrilled, and who would have made him most thrill, to its deepest and highest meaning. Green grass and summer roses were waving over the earth that had shut in all dreams like these, for him. As he wandered about, he had told himself that he had been mad to come and see it all, so alone. Sometimes he turned away from the crowd, and sat in some quiet corner of palace or fairy garden; and it was because he was forced to do it, for it was at times when he was in no condition to be looked at by careless passers-by.

He had never been particularly fond of children; but somehow these two waifs, with their alert faces and odd independence, had wakened his interest. He was con-

scious of rather wanting to know where they had come
from and what they would do next. The bit of the story
of the Genius of the Palace of the Sea had attracted him.
He had learned to love stories from the one who should
have seen with him the Enchanted City. She had been a
story lover, and full of fancies.

He followed the trio to the end of the great Court.
When they reached there, three pairs of cheeks were
flushed, and the eyes that were open were glowing. Meg
and Robin chose a spot of ground, and stopped.

"Now," said Meg, "open them—suddenly!"

The boy opened them. The man saw the look that
flashed into his face. It was a strange, quivering look.
Palaces, which seemed of pure marble, surrounded him.
He had never even dreamed of palaces. White stairways
rose from the lagoon, leading to fair, open portals the wondering world passed through to splendors held within. A
great statue of gold towered noble and marvellous, with
uplifted arms holding high the emblems of its spirit and
power, and at the end of this vista, through the archway,
and between the line of columns, bearing statues poised
against the background of sky, he caught glimpses of the
lake's scintillating blue.

He uttered a weird little sound. It was part exclama-
tion, and a bit of a laugh, cut short by something like a
nervous sob, which did not know what to do with itself.

"Oh!" he said. And then, "Oh!" again. And then

"I—I don't know—what it's—like!" And he cleared his throat and stared, and Meg saw his narrow chest heave up and down.

"It isn't *like* anything, but—but something we've dreamed of, perhaps," said Meg, gazing in ecstasy with him.

"No—no!" answered Ben. "But I've never dreamed like it."

Meg put her hand on his shoulder.

"But you will now," she said. "You will now."

And their man had been near enough to hear, and he came to them.

"Good morning," he said. "You're having another day of it, I see."

Meg and Robin looked up at him, radiant. They were both in good enough mood to make friends. They felt friends with everybody.

"Good morning," they answered; and Robin added, "We're going to come every day as long as we can make our money last."

"That's a good enough idea," said their man. "Where are your father and mother?"

Meg lifted her solemn, black-lashed eyes to his. She was noticing again about the dreary look in his face.

"They died nearly four years ago," she answered, for Robin.

"Who is with you?" asked the man, meeting her

questioning gaze with a feeling that her great eyes were oddly thoughtful for a child's, and that there was a look in them he had seen before in a pair of eyes closed a year ago. It gave him an almost startled feeling.

"Nobody is with us," Meg said, "except Ben."

"You came alone?" said the man.

"Yes."

He looked at her for a moment in silence, and then turned away and looked across the Court to where the lake gleamed through the colonnade.

"So did I," he said, reflectively. "So did I. Quite alone."

Meg and Robin glanced at each other.

"Yesterday Rob and I came by ourselves," said Meg next, and she said it gently. "But we were not lonely; and to-day we have Ben."

The man turned his eyes on the boy.

"You're Ben, are you?" he said.

"Yes," Ben answered. "And but for them I couldn't never have seen it—never!"

"Why?" the man asked. "Almost everybody can see it."

"But not me," said Ben. "And I wanted to more than any one—seemed like to me. And when they roomed at our house last night, mother was going to give me the fifty cents, but—but father—father, he took it away from us. And they brought me."

Then the man turned on Robin.

"Have you plenty of money?" he asked, unceremoniously.

"No," said Rob.

"They're as poor as I am," put in Ben. "They couldn't afford to room anywhere but with poor people."

"But everybody—" Meg began impulsively, and then stopped, remembering that it was not Robin she was talking to.

"But everybody—what?" said the man.

It was Robin who answered for her this time.

"She said that last night," he explained, with a half shy laugh, "that everybody had something they could give to somebody else."

"Oh, well, it isn't always money, of course, or anything big," said Meg, hurriedly. "It might be something that is ever so little."

The man laughed, but his eyes seemed to be remembering something as he looked over the lagoon again.

"That's a pretty good thing to think," he said. "Now," turning on Meg rather suddenly, "I wonder what you have to give to *me*."

"I don't know," she answered, perhaps a trifle wistfully. "The thing I give to Rob and Ben is a very little one."

"She makes up things to tell us about the places we can't pay to go into, or don't understand," said Robin. "It's not as little as she thinks it is."

"Well," said the man, "look here! Perhaps that's what you have to give to me. You came to this place alone and so did I. I believe you're enjoying yourselves more than I am. You're going to take Ben about and tell him stories. Suppose you take me!"

"You!" Meg exclaimed. "But you're a man, and you know all about it, I dare say; and I only tell things I make up—fairy stories, and other things. A man wouldn't care for them. He—he knows."

"He knows too much, perhaps—that's the trouble," said the man. "A fairy or so might do me good. I'm not acquainted enough with them. And if I know things you don't—perhaps that's what I have to give to *you*."

"Why," said Meg, her eyes growing as she looked up at his odd, clever face, "do you want to go about with us?"

"Yes," said the man, with a quick, decided nod, "I believe that's just what I want to do. I'm lonelier than you two. At least, you are together. Come on, children," but it was to Meg he held out his hand. "Take me with you."

And, bewildered as she was, Meg found herself giving her hand to him and being led away, Robin and Ben close beside them.

"TAKE ME WITH YOU."

XVI

IT was such a strange thing—so unlike the things of every day, and so totally an unexpected thing, that for a little while they all three had a sense of scarcely knowing what to do with themselves. If Robin and Meg had not somehow rather liked the man, and vaguely felt him friendly, and if there had not been in their impressionable minds that fancy about his being far from as happy as the other people of the crowds looked, it is more than probable that they would not have liked their position, and would have felt that it might spoil their pleasure.

But they were sympathetic children, and they had been lonely and sad enough themselves to be moved by a sadness in others, even if it was an uncomprehended one.

As she walked by the man's side, still letting her hand remain in his, Meg kept giving him scrutinizing looks aside, and trying in her way to read him. He was a man just past middle life, he was powerful and well-built, and had keen, and at the same time rather unhappy-looking, blue eyes, with brows and lashes as black as Rob's and her own. There was something strong in his fine-looking, clean-shaven face, and the hand which held hers had a good, firm grasp, and felt like a hand which had worked in its time.

As for the man himself, he was trying an experiment.
He had been suddenly seized with a desire to try it, and see
how it would result.   He was not sure that it would be a
success, but if it proved one it might help to rid him of
gloom he would be glad to be relieved of.   He felt it rather
promising when Meg went at once to the point and asked
him a practical question.

"You don't know our names?" she said.

"You don't know mine," he answered.   "It's John Holt.
You can call me that."

"John Holt," said Meg.   "Mr. John Holt."

The man laughed.   Her grave, practical little air pleased
him.

"Say John Holt, without the handle to it," he said.   "It
sounds well."

Meg looked at him inquiringly.   Though he had
laughed, he seemed to mean what he said.

"It's queer, of course," she said, "because we don't
know each other well; but I can do it, if you like."

"I do like," he said, and he laughed again.

"Very well," said Meg.   "My name's Margaret Macleod,
I'm called Meg for short.   My brother's name is Robin, and
Ben's is Ben Nowell.   Where shall we go first?"

"You are the leader of the party," he answered, his face
beginning to brighten a little.   "Where shall it be?"

"The Palace of the Genius of the Flowers," she said.

"Is that what it is called?" he asked.

"That's what we call it," she explained. "That's part of the fairy story. *We* are part of a fairy story, and all these are palaces that the Genii built for the Great Magician."

"That's first-rate," he said. "Just tell us about it. Ben and I have not heard."

At first she had wondered if she could tell her stories to a grown-up person, but there was something in his voice and face that gave her the feeling that she could. She laughed a little when she began ; but he listened with enjoyment that was so plain, and Ben, walking by her side, looked up with such eager, enraptured, and wondering eyes, that she went on bravely. It grew, as stories will, in being told, and it was better than it had been the day before. Robin himself saw that, and leaned towards her as eagerly as Ben.

By the time they entered the Palace of the Flowers and stood among the flame of colors, and beneath the great palm fronds swaying under the crystal globe that was its dome, she had warmed until she was all aglow, and as full of fancies as the pavilions were of blossoms.

As she dived into the story of the Genius who strode through tropical forests and deep jungles, over purple moors and up mountain sides, where strange-hued pale or vivid things grew in tangles, or stood in the sun alone, John Holt became of the opinion that his experiment would be a success. It was here that he began to find he had gifts to give. She asked him questions ; Robin and Ben asked

him questions; the three drew close to him, and hung on
his every word.

"You know the things and the places where they grow,"
Meg said. "We have never seen anything. We can only
try to imagine. You can tell us." And he did tell them;
and as they went from court to pavilion, surrounded by
sumptuous bloom and sumptuous leafage and sumptuous
fragrance, the three beginning to cling to him, to turn to
him with every new discovery, and to forget he was a
stranger, he knew that he was less gloomy than he had been
before, and that somehow this thing seemed worth doing.

And in this way they went from place to place. As
they had seen beauties and wonders the day before, they
saw wonders and beauties to-day, but to-day their pleasure
had a flavor new to them. For the first time in years, since
they had left their little seat at their own fireside, they were
not alone, and some one seemed to mean to look after
them. John Holt was an eminently practical person, and
when they left the Palace of the Flowers they began
vaguely to realize that, stranger or not, he had taken charge
of them. It was evident that he was in the habit of taking
charge of people and things. He took charge of the
satchel. It appeared that he knew where it was safe to
leave it.

"Can we get it at lunch time?" Robin asked, with some
anxiety.

"You can get it when you want it," said John Holt.

A little later he looked at Ben's pale, small face scrutinizingly.

"Look here," he said, "you're tired." And without any further question he called up a rolling-chair.

"Get into that," he said.

"Me?" said Ben, a little alarmed.

"Yes."

And, almost a shade paler at the thought of such grandeur, Ben got in, and fell back with a luxurious sigh.

And at midday, when they were beginning to feel ravenous, though no one mentioned the subject, he asked Meg a blunt question.

"Where did you eat your lunch yesterday?" he asked.

Meg flushed a little, feeling that hospitality demanded that they should share the remaining eggs with such a companion, and she was afraid there would be very few to offer, when Ben was taken into consideration.

"We went to a quiet place on the Wooded Island," she said, "and ate it with the roses. We pretended they invited us. We had only hard-boiled eggs and a sandwich each; but a kind woman gave us something of her own."

"We brought the eggs from home," explained Rob. "We have some chickens of our own, who laid them. We thought that would be cheaper than buying things."

"Oh!" said John Holt. "So you've been living on hard-boiled eggs. Got any left?"

"A few," Meg answered.   "They're in the satchel.   We shall have to go and get it."

"Come along, then," said John Holt.   "Pretty hungry by this time, aren't you?"

"Yes," said Meg, with heartfelt frankness, "we are!"

It was astonishing how much John Holt had found out about them during this one morning.   They did not know themselves how much their answers to his occasional questions had told him.   He had not known himself, when he asked the questions, how much their straightforward, practical replies would reveal.   They had not sentimentalized over their friendless loneliness, but he had found himself realizing what desolate, unnoticed, and uncared-for things their lives were.   They had not told him how they had tired their young bodies with work too heavy for them, but he had realized it.   In his mind there had risen a picture of the Straw Parlor, under the tent-like roof of the barn, with these two huddled together in the cold, buried in the straw, while they talked over their desperate plans.   They had never thought of calling themselves strong and determined, and clear of wit, but he knew how strong and firm of purpose and endurance two creatures so young and unfriended, and so poor, must have been to form a plan so bold, and carry it out in the face of the obstacles of youth and inexperience, and empty pockets and hands.   He had laughed at the story of the Treasure saved in pennies, and hidden deep in the straw; but as he had laughed he had

thought, with a quick, soft throb of his heart, that the woman he had loved and lost would have laughed with him, with tears in the eyes which Meg's reminded him of. He somehow felt as if she might be wandering about with them in their City Beautiful this morning, they were so entirely creatures she would have been drawn to, and longed to make happier.

He liked their fancy of making their poor little feast within scent of the roses. It was just such a fancy as She might have had herself. And he wanted to see what they had to depend on. He knew it must be little, and it touched him to know that, little as they had, they meant to share it with their poorer friend.

They went for the satchel, and when they did so they began to calculate as to what they could add to its contents. They were few things, and poor ones.

He did not sit down, but stood by and watched them for a moment, when, having reached their sequestered nook, they began to spread out their banquet. It was composed of the remnant eggs, some bread, and a slice of cheese. It looked painfully scant, and Meg had an anxious eye.

"Is that all?" asked John Holt, abruptly.

"Yes," said Meg. "We shall have to make it do."

"My Lord!" ejaculated John Holt, suddenly, in his blunt fashion. And he turned round and walked away.

"Where's he gone?" exclaimed Ben, timidly.

But they none of them could guess. Nice as he had

been, he had a brusque way, and, perhaps, he meant to leave them.

But by the time they had divided the eggs, and the bread and cheese, and had fairly begun, he came marching back. He had a basket on his arm, and two bottles stuck out of one coat pocket, while a parcel protruded from the other. He came and threw himself down on the grass beside them, and opened the basket. It was full of good things.

"I'm going to have lunch with you," he said, "and I have a pretty big appetite, so I've brought you something to eat. You can't tramp about on that sort of thing."

The basket they had seen the day before had been a poor thing compared to this. The contents of this would have been a feast for much more fastidious creatures than three ravenous children. There were chickens and sandwiches and fruit; the bottles held lemonade, and the package in the coat pocket was a box of candy.

"We—never had such good things in our lives," Meg gasped, amazed.

"Hadn't you?" said John Holt, with a kind, and even a happy, grin. "Well, pitch in."

XVII

WHAT a feast it was—what a feast! They were so hungry, they were so happy, they were so rejoiced! And John Holt watched them as if he had never enjoyed himself so much before. He laughed, he made jokes, he handed out good things, he poured out lemonade.

"Let's drink to the Great Magician!" he said, filling the little glasses he had brought; and he made them drink it standing, as a toast. In all the grounds that day there was no such a party, it was so exhilarated and amazed at itself. Little Ben looked and ate and laughed as if the lemonade had gone to his head.

"Oh, my!" he said, "if mother could see me!"

"We'll bring her to-morrow," said John Holt.

"Are you—" faltered Meg, looking at him with wide eyes, "are you coming again to-morrow?"

"Yes," John Holt answered, "and you are coming with me; and we'll come every day until you've seen it all—if you three will pilot me around."

"You must be very rich, John Holt," said Meg. She had found out that it was his whim to want her to call him so.

"I have plenty of money," he said, "if that's being rich. Oh, yes, I've got money enough! I've more land than Aunt Matilda."

And then it was that suddenly Robin remembered something.

"I believe," he said, "that I've heard Aunt Matilda speak about you to Jones. I seem to remember your name. You have the biggest farm in Illinois, and you have houses and houses in town. Meg, don't you remember—when he got married, and everybody talked about how rich he was?"

And Meg did remember. She looked at him softly, and thought she knew why he had seemed gloomy, for she remembered that this rich and envied man's wife had had a little child and died suddenly. And she had even heard once that it had almost driven him mad, because he had been fond of her.

"Are you—that one?" she said.

"Yes," he answered, "I'm the one who got married." And the cloud fell on his face again, and for a minute or so rested there. For he thought this thing which had happened to him was cruel and hideous, and he had never ceased to rebel against it bitterly.

Meg drew a little closer to him, but she said no more about what she knew he was thinking of. She was a clever little thing, and knew this was not the time.

And after they had eaten of the good things, until hunger seemed a thing of the past, the afternoon began as

a fairy story, indeed. Little by little they began to realize that John Holt was their good and powerful giant, for it seemed that he was not only ready to do everything for them, but was rich enough.

"Have you been to the Midway Plaisance?" he asked them. He felt very sure, however, that they had not, or that, if they had, with that scant purse, they had not seen what they longed to see.

"No, we haven't," said Meg. "We thought we would save it until we had seen so many other things that we should not mind so *very* much only seeing the outsides of places. We knew we should have to make up stories all the time."

"We won't save it," said John Holt. "We'll go now. We will hobnob with Bedouins and Japanese and Turks, and shake hands with Amazons and Indians; we'll ride on camels and go to the Chinese Theatre. Come along."

And to this Arabian Nights' Entertainment he took them all. They felt as if he were a prince. And oh, the exciting strangeness of it! To be in such a place and amid such marvels, with a man who seemed to set no limit to the resources of his purse. They never had been even near a person who spent money as if it were made for spending, and the good things of life were made to be bought by it. What John Holt spent was only what other people with full purses spent in the Midway Plaisance, but to Meg and Robin and Ben it seemed that he poured forth money in

torrents. They looked at him with timorous wonder and marvelling gratitude. It seemed that he meant them to see everything and to do everything. They rode on camels down a street in Cairo, they talked to chiefs of the desert, they listened to strange music, they heard strange tongues, and tasted strange confections. Robin and Ben went about like creatures in a delightful dream. Every few minutes during the first hour Robin would sidle close to Meg, and clutch her dress or her hand with a gasp of rapture.

"Oh, Meg!" he would say, "and yesterday we were so poor! And now we are seeing *everything!*"

And when John Holt heard him, he would laugh half to himself; a laugh with a touch of pleasant exultation in it, and no gloom at all. He had found something to distract him at last.

He liked to watch Meg's face, as they went from one weirdly foreign place to another. Her eyes were immense with delight, and her face had the flush of an Indian peach. Once she stopped suddenly, in such a glow of strange delight that her eyes were full of other brightness than the shining of her pleasure.

"Fairy stories *do* happen!" she said. "You have made one! It was a fairy story yesterday—but *now*—oh! just think how like a fairy king you are, and what you are giving to us! It will be enough to make stories of forever!"

He laughed again. She found out in time that he often

laughed that short half-laugh when he was moved by something. He had had a rough sort of life, successful as it had been, and it was not easy for him to express all he felt.

"That's all right," he said, "that's just as it should be. But you are giving something to me, too—you three."

And so they were, and it was not a little thing.

Their afternoon was a thing of which they could never have dreamed and for which they could never have hoped. Before it was half over they began to feel that not only John Holt was a prince, but that by some magic meta-morphosis they had become princes themselves. It seemed that nothing in that City Beautiful was to be closed to them. It was John Holt's habit to do things in a thorough, business-like way, and he did this thing in a manner which was a credit to his wit and good sense.

Ben, who had never been taken care of in his life, was taken about in a chair, and looked after in a way that made him wonder if he were not dreaming, and if he should not be wakened presently by the sound of his father's drunken voice.

Robin found himself more than once rubbing his fore-head in a puzzled fashion.

Meg felt rather as if she had become a princess. Some-how, she and John Holt seemed to have known each other a long time. He seemed to like to keep her near him, and

always kept his eye on her, to see if she was enjoying herself, and was comfortable, or tired. She found herself being wheeled by Ben, when John Holt decided it was time for her to rest. He walked by her and talked to her, answering all her questions. More than once it flashed into her mind that it would be very awful when all this joy was over, and they parted, as they would. But they were going to see him to-morrow, he had said.

It seemed as if they marched from one climax of new experience to another.

"You're going to dine with me," he announced. "You've had enough hard-boiled eggs. And we'll see the illuminations afterwards."

He took them to what seemed to them a dining-place for creatures of another world, it was so brilliant with light, so decorated, so gorgeous. Servants moved to and fro, electric globes gleamed, palms and flowers added to the splendor of color and brightness. John Holt gave them an excellent dinner ; they thought it was a banquet. Ben kept his eyes on John Holt's face at every mouthful—he felt as if he might vanish away. He looked as if he had done this every day of his life. He called the waiters as if he knew no awe of any human being, and the waiters flew to obey him.

In the evening he took them to see the City Beautiful as it looked at night. It was set, it seemed to them, with myriads of diamonds, all alight. Endless chains of jewels seemed strung and wound about it. The Palace of the

Flowers held up a great crystal of light glowing against the dark blue of the sky, towers and domes were crowned and diademed, thousands of jewels hung among the masses of leaves, or reflected themselves, sparkling, in the darkness of the lagoons, fountains of molten jewels sprung up, and flamed and changed. The City Beautiful stood out whiter and more spirit-like than ever, in the pure radiance of these garlands of clearest flame.

When first they came out upon it Robin involuntarily pressed close to Meg, and their twin hands clasped each other.

"Oh, Meg!" cried Robin.

"Oh, Robin!" breathed Meg, and she turned to John Holt and caught his hand too.

"Oh, John Holt!" she said; "John Holt!"

Very primitive and brief exclamations of joy, but somehow human beings have uttered them just as simply in all great moments through centuries.

John Holt knew just the degree of rapturous feeling they expressed, and he held Meg's hand close and with a warm grasp.

They saw the marvellous fairy spectacle from all points and from all sides. Led by John Holt, they lost no view and no beauty. They feasted full of all the delight of it; and at last he took them to a quiet corner, where, through the trees, sparkled lights and dancing water, and let them talk it out.

The day had been such an incredible one, with its succession of excitements and almost unreal pleasures, that they had actually forgotten that the night must come. They were young enough for that indiscretion, and when they sat down and began to realize how tired they were, they also began to realize a number of other things.

A little silence fell upon them. Ben's head began to droop slightly upon his shoulder, and John Holt's quick eye saw it.

"Have you had a good day?" he asked.

"Rob," said Meg, "when we sat in the Straw Parlor and talked about the City Beautiful, and the people who would come to it—when we thought we could never see it ourselves—did we ever dream that anybody—even if they were kings and queens—could have such a day?"

"Never," answered Robin; "never! We didn't know such a day was in the world."

"That's right," said John Holt. "I'm glad it's seemed as good as that. Now, where did you think of spending the night?"

Meg and Rob looked at each other. Since Rob had suggested to her in the morning a bold thought, they had had no time to discuss the matter, but now each one remembered the bold idea. Rob got up and came close to John Holt.

"This morning I thought of something," he said, "and once again this afternoon I thought of it. I don't know

whether we could do it, but you could tell us. Do you think—this is such a big place and there are so many corners we could creep into, and it's such a fine night—do you think we could wait until all the people are gone and then find a place to sleep without going out of the grounds? It would save us buying the tickets in the morning, and Ben could stay with us—I told his mother that perhaps he might not come home—and he could have another day."

John Holt laughed his short laugh.

"Were you thinking of doing that?" he said. "Well, you have plenty of sand, anyway."

"Do you think we could do it?" asked Meg. "Would they find us and drive us out?"

John Holt laughed again.

"Great Cæsar!" he said, "no; I don't think they'd find you two. Luck would be with you. But I know a plan worth two of that. I'm going to take you all three to my hotel."

"A hotel?" said Meg.

Ben lifted his sleepy head from his shoulder.

"Yes," said John Holt. "I can make them find corners for you, though they're pretty crowded. I'm not going to lose sight of you. This has begun to be *my* tea-party."

Meg looked at him with large and solemn eyes.

"Well," she said, "it's a fairy story, and it's getting fairyer and fairyer every minute."

She leaned forward, with her heart quite throbbing. Because it was he who did this splendid thing—he to whom all things seemed possible—it actually seemed a thing to be accepted as if a magician had done it.

"Oh, how good you are to us!" she said. "How good, and how good! And what is the use of saying only 'Thank you'? I should not be surprised," with a touch of awe, "if you took us to a hotel built of *gold*."

How heartily John Holt laughed then.

"Well, some of them ought to be, by the time this thing's over," he said. "But the lights will soon be out; the people are going, and Ben's nearly dead. Let's go and find a carriage."

XVIII

YES, they went home in a carriage! John Holt put them into it, and settled back into it himself, as if comfortable cushions were only what belonged to tired people. And he took them to one of the hotels whose brilliantly lighted fronts they had trudged wearily by the night before. And they had a good supper and warm baths and delicious beds, and Meg went to sleep with actual tears of wonder and gratitude on her lashes, and they all three slept the sleep of Eden and dreamed the dreams of Paradise. And in the morning they had breakfast with John Holt, in the hotel dining-room, and a breakfast as good as the princely dinner he had given them; and after it they all went back with him to the City Beautiful, and the fairy story began again. For near the entrance where they went in they actually found Ben's mother, in a state of wonder beyond words; for, by the use of some magic messenger, that wonderful John Holt had sent word to her that Ben was in safe hands, and that she must come and join him, and the money to make this possible had been in the letter.

Poor, tired, discouraged, down-trodden woman, how she lost her breath when Ben threw himself upon her and poured

forth his story! And what a face she wore through all that followed! How Ben led her from triumph to triumph, with the exultant air of one to whom the City Beautiful almost belonged, and who, consequently, had it to bestow as a rich gift on those who did not know it as he did. What wondering glances his mother kept casting on his face, which had grown younger with each hour! She had never seen him look like this before. And what glances she cast aside at John Holt! This was one of the rich men poor people heard of. She had never been near one of them. She had, often, rather hated them.

Before the day was over Robin and Meg realized that this wonder was to go on as long as there was anything of the City Beautiful they had not seen. They were to drink deep draughts of delight as long as they were thirsty for more. John Holt made this plain to them in his blunt, humorous way. He was going to show them everything and share all their pleasures, and they were to stay at the golden hotel every night.

And John Holt was getting almost as much out of it as they were. He wandered about alone no more; he did not feel as if he were only a ghost, with nothing in common with the human beings passing by. In the interest and excitement of generalship and management, and the amusement of seeing this unspoiled freshness of his charges' delight in all things, the gloomy look faded out of his face, and he looked like a different man. Once they came

upon two men who seemed to know him, and the first one who spoke to him glanced at the children in some surprise.

"Hallo, John!" he said, "set up a family?"

"Just what I've done," answered John Holt. "Set up a family. A man's no right to be going around a place like this without one."

"How do you get on with it?" asked the other. "Find it pay?"

"Pay!" said John Holt, with a big laugh. "Great Scott! I should say so! It's worth twice the price of admission!"

"Glad of it," said his friend, giving him a curious look.

And as he went away Meg heard him say to his companion,

"It was time he found something that paid — John Holt. He was in a pretty bad way—a *pretty* bad way."

As they became more and more intimate, and spoke more to each other, Meg understood how bad a "way" he had been in. She was an observing, old-fashioned child, and she saw many things a less sympathetic creature might have passed by; and when John Holt discovered this— which he was quite shrewd enough to do rather soon—he gradually began to say things to her he would not have said to other people. She understood, somehow, that, though the black look passed away from his face, and

he laughed and made them laugh, there was a thing that
was never quite out of his mind. She saw that pictures
brought it back to him, that strains of music did, that
pretty mothers with children hurt him when they passed,
and that every now and then he would cast a broad glance
over all the whiteness and blueness and beauty and grace,
and draw a long, quick sigh—as if he were homesick for
something.

"You know," he said once, when he did this and looked
round, and found Meg's eyes resting yearningly upon him,
"you know She was coming with me! We planned it all.
Lord! how She liked to talk of it! She said it would be
an Enchanted City—just as you did, Meg. That was one
of the first things that made me stop to listen—when I
heard you say that. An Enchanted City!" he repeated,
pondering. "Lord, Lord!"

"Well," said Meg, with a little catch in her breath,
"well, you know, John Holt, she's got to an Enchanted
City that won't vanish away, hasn't she?"

She did not say it with any sanctified little air. Out
of their own loneliness, and the "Pilgrim's Progress," and
her ardent fancies, the place she and Robin had built to
take refuge in was a very real thing. It had many modern
improvements upon the vagueness of harps and crowns.
There were good souls who might have been astounded
and rather shocked by it, but the children believed in it
very implicitly, and found great comfort in their confidence

in its joyfulness. They thought of themselves as walking about its streets exactly as rapturously as they walked about this earthly City Beautiful. And because it was so real there was a note in Meg's voice which gave John Holt a sudden touch of new feeling, as he looked back at her.

"Do you suppose she is?" he said. "You believe in that, don't you—you believe in it?"

Meg looked a little troubled for a moment.

"Why," she said, "Rob and I talk to each other and invent things about it, just as we talked about this. We just *have* to, you see. Perhaps we say things that would seem very funny to religious people—I don't think we're religious—but—but we do *like* it."

"Do you?" said John Holt. "Perhaps I should, too. You shall tell me some stories about it, and you shall put Her there. If I could feel as if she were somewhere!"

"Oh," said Meg, "she must be somewhere, you know. She couldn't *go out*, John Holt."

He cast his broad glance all around, and caught his breath, as if remembering.

"Lord, Lord!" he said. "No! *She* couldn't go out!"

Meg knew afterwards why he said this with such force. "She" had been a creature who was so full of life, and of the joy of living. She had been gay, and full of laughter and humor. She had had a wonderful, vivid mind, which found color and feeling and story in the commonest things.

She had been so clever and so witty, and such a bright and warm thing in her house. When she had gone away from earth so suddenly, people had said, with wonder, "But it seemed as if she *could* not die!" But she had died, and her child had died too, scarcely an hour after it was born, and John Holt had been left stunned and aghast, and almost stricken into gloomy madness. And in some way Meg was like her, with her vivid little face and her black-lashed eyes, her City Beautiful and her dreams and stories, which made the realities of her life. It was a strange chance, a marvellously kind chance, which had thrown them together; these two, who were of such different worlds, and yet, who needed each other so much.

During the afternoon, seeing that Meg looked a little tired, and also realizing, in his practical fashion, that Ben's mother would be more at ease in the society she was used to, John Holt sent her to ramble about with her boy, and Robin went with them; and Meg and John went to rest with the thousands of roses among the bowers of the fairy island, and there they said a good deal to each other. John Holt seemed to get a kind of comfort in finding words for some of the thoughts he had been silent about in the past.

"It's a queer thing," he said, "but when I talk to you about her I feel as if she were somewhere near."

"Perhaps she is," said Meg, in her matter-of-fact little way. "We don't know what they are doing. But if you

had gone into another world, and she had stayed here, you know you would have come to take care of her."

"That's true," said John Holt. "I took care of her when she was here, the Lord knows. There wasn't anything on earth she liked that I wouldn't have broken my neck to get at. When I built that house for her—I built a big house to take her to when we were married—she said I hadn't left out a thing she cared for. And she *knew* what things ought to be. She wasn't like me, Meg. I'd spent my life trying to make a fortune. I began when I was a boy, and I worked hard. She belonged to people with money, and she'd read books and travelled and seen things. She knew it all. I didn't, when first I knew her, but I learned fast enough afterwards. I couldn't help it while I was with her. We planned the house together. It was one of the best in the country—architecture, furniture, pictures, and all the rest. The first evening we spent there——" He stopped and cleared his throat, and was silent a few seconds. Then he added, in a rather unsteady voice, "We were pretty happy people that evening."

Later he showed Meg her miniature. He carried it in an oval case in his inside pocket. It was the picture of a young woman with a brilliant face, lovely laughing eyes, and a bright, curving red mouth.

"No," he said, as he looked at it, "She *couldn't* go out. She's somewhere."

Then he told Meg about the rooms they had made ready

for "John Holt, Junior," as they had called the little child who died so quickly.

"It was her idea," he said.   "There was a nursery, with picture paper on the walls.   There was a bathroom, with tiles that told stories about little mermen and mermaids, that she had made up herself.   There was a bedroom, with a swinging cot, frilled with lace and tied with ribbons.   And there were picture-books and toys.   The doors never were opened.   John Holt, Junior, never slept in his cot.   He slept with his mother."

There he broke off a moment again.

"She used to be sorry he wouldn't be old enough to appreciate all this," he said next.   "She used to laugh about him, and say, he was going to be cheated out of it.   But she said he should come with us, so that he could say he had been.   She said he had to see it, if he only stared at it and said 'goo.'"

"Perhaps he does see it," said Meg.   "I should think those who have got away from here, and know more what being alive really means, would want to see what earth people are *trying* to do—though they know so little."

"That sounds pretty good," said John Holt ; "I like that."

They had been seated long enough to feel rested, and they rose and went on their way, to begin their pilgrimage again.   Just as they were crossing the bridge they saw Robin coming tearing towards them.   He evidently had left

Ben and his mother somewhere. He was alone. His hat was on the back of his head, and he was hot with running.

"Something has happened," said Meg, "and I believe I know——"

But Robin had reached them.

"Meg," he said, panting for breath, "Aunt Matilda's here! She didn't see me, but I saw her. She's in the Agricultural Building, standing before a new steam plough, and she's chewing a sample of wheat."

XIX

THE two children did not know exactly whether they were frightened or not. If it had not seemed impossible that anything should go entirely wrong while John Holt was near them, they would have felt rather queer. But John Holt was evidently not the least alarmed.

"Look here," he said, "I'm glad of it. I want to see that woman."

"Do you?" exclaimed Robin and Meg together.

"Yes, I do," he said. "Come along, and let's go and find her." And he strode out towards the Agricultural Building as if he were going towards something interesting.

It is true that the Agricultural Building had been too nearly connected with Aunt Matilda's world to hold the greatest attractions for the little Pilgrims. It had, indeed, gone rather hard with them to find a name for it with a beautiful sound.

"But it *is* something," Meg had said, "and it's a great, huge thing, whether we care for it or not. That it isn't the thing we care for doesn't make it any less. We should be fools if we thought that, of course. And you know we're not fools, Rob."

"No," Rob had said, standing gazing at rakes and

harrows with his brows knit and his legs pretty wide apart. "And if there's one thing that shows human beings *can* do what they set their minds to, it's this place. Why, they used to thresh wheat with flails — two pieces of wood hooked together. They banged the wheat on the barn floor with things like that! I'll tell you what, as soon as a man gets any sense, he begins to make machines. He bangs at things with his brain, instead of with his arms and legs."

And in the end they had called it the Palace of the Genius of the Earth, and the Seasons, and the Sun. They walked manfully by John Holt through the place, Robin leading the way, until they came to the particular exhibit where he had caught sight of Aunt Matilda. Being a business-like and thorough person, she was still there, though she had left the steam plough and directed her attention to a side-delivery hay rake, which she seemed to find very well worth study.

If the children and John Holt had not walked up and planted themselves immediately in her path, she would not have seen them. It gave Meg a little shudder to see how like her world she looked, with her hard, strong-featured face, her straight skirt, and her square shoulders. They waited until she moved, and then she looked up and saw them. She did not start or look nervous in the least. She stared at them.

"Well," she said. "So this was the place you came to."

"Yes, Aunt Matilda," said Robin. "We couldn't let it go by us—and we took our own money."

"And we knew you wouldn't be anxious about us," said Meg, looking up at her with a shade of curiosity.

Aunt Matilda gave a dry laugh.

"No," she said, "I've no time to be anxious about children. I took care of myself when I was your age ; and I had a sort of notion you'd come here. Who are you with ?"

John Holt lifted his hat, but without too much ceremony. He knew Mrs. Matilda Jennings's principles were opposed to the ceremonious.

"I'm a sort of neighbor of yours, Mrs. Jennings," he explained. "I have some land near your farm, though I don't live on the place. My name is John Holt."

Aunt Matilda glanced from him to Robin.

She knew all about John Holt, and was quite sufficiently business-like to realize that it would be considered good luck to have him for a friend.

"Well," she said to them, "you've got into good hands."

John Holt laughed.

"By this time we all three think we've got into good hands," he said ; "and we're going to see this thing through."

"They haven't money enough to see much of it," said Mrs. Jennings.

"No," said John Holt, "but I have, and it's to be my treat."

"Well," said Aunt Matilda, "I suppose you can afford it. I couldn't. I've come here on business."

"You'd better let us help you to combine a little pleasure with it," said John Holt. "This won't happen twice in your life or mine."

"There's been a lot of money wasted in decorations," said Mrs. Jennings. "I don't believe it will pay them."

"Oh, yes; it will pay them," said John Holt. "It would pay them if they didn't make a cent out of it. It would have paid *me*, if I'd done it, and lost money."

"Now, see here," said Mrs. Matilda Jennings, with a shrewd air, "the people that built this didn't do it for their health—they did it for what they'd make out of it."

"Perhaps they did," said John Holt, "and perhaps all of them didn't. And even those that did have made a bigger thing than they knew, by Jupiter!"

They were all sauntering along together, as they spoke. Meg and Robin wondered what John Holt was going to do. It looked rather as if he wanted to see more of Aunt Matilda. And it proved that he did. He had a reason of his own, and, combined with this, a certain keen sense of humor made her entertaining to him. He wanted to see how the place affected her, as he had wanted to look on at its effect on Meg and Robin. But he knew that Aunt Matilda had come to accumulate new ideas on agriculture, and that

she must be first allowed to satisfy herself on that point; and he knew the children were not specially happy in the society of ploughs and threshing-machines, and he did not think Aunt Matilda's presence would add to their pleasure in the Palace of the Earth, the Seasons, and the Sun. Besides, he wanted to talk to Mrs. Jennings a little alone.

"You know where Ben and his mother are?" he said to Robin, after a few minutes.

"Yes," Robin answered.

"Then take Meg and go to them for a while. Mrs. Jennings wants to stay here about an hour more, and I want to walk round with her. In an hour come back to the entrance here and I will meet you."

Meg and Robin went away as he told them. It was in one sense rather a relief.

"I wonder what she'll say to him," said Meg.

"There's no knowing," Robin answered. "But whatever it is, he will make it all right. He's one of those who have found out human beings can do things if they try hard enough. He was as lonely and poor as we are when he was twelve. He told me so."

What Aunt Matilda said was very matter-of-fact.

"I must say," she said, as the children walked off, "you seem to have been pretty good to them."

"They've been pretty good to me," said John Holt. "They've been pretty good *for* me, though they're not old enough to know it."

"They're older than their age," said Aunt Matilda. "If they'd been like other children the Lord knows what I should have done with them. They've been no trouble in particular."

"I should imagine not," said John Holt.

"It was pretty business-like of them," said Mrs. Jennings, with another dry laugh, "to make up their minds without saying a word to any one, and just hustle around and make their money to come here. They both worked pretty steady, I can tell you, and it wasn't easy work, either. Most young ones would have given in. But they were bound to get here."

"They'll be bound to get pretty much where they make up their minds to, as life goes on," remarked John Holt. "That's their build."

"Thank goodness, they're not like their father," Mrs. Jennings commented. "Robert hadn't any particular fault, but he never made anything."

"He and his wife seem to have made a home that was a pretty good start for these children," was what John Holt said.

"Well," said Mrs. Jennings, "they've got to do the rest themselves. He left them nothing."

"No other relations but you?" John Holt asked.

"Not a soul. I shall keep them and let them work on the farm, I suppose."

"It would pay to educate them well and let them see the world," said John Holt.

"I dare say it would pay *them*," replied Aunt Matilda, "but I've got all I can do, and my husband's family have a sort of claim on me. Half the farm belonged to him."

They spent their remaining hours in the Agricultural Building very profitably. Mrs. Jennings found John Holt an excellent companion. He knew things very thoroughly, and had far-seeing ideas of how far things would work, and how much they would pay. He did not expect Mrs. Jennings to tell him fairy stories, and he told her none, but before they left the place they had talked a good deal. John Holt had found out all he wanted to know about the two children, and he had made a proposition which certainly gave Aunt Matilda something new to think of.

She was giving some thought to it when they went out to meet the party of four at the entrance. She looked as if she had been rather surprised by some occurrence, but she did not look displeased, and the glances she gave to Meg and Robin expressed a new sense of appreciation of their practical value.

"I've promised Mr. Holt that I'll let him take me through the Midway Plaisance," she said. "I've seen the things I came to see, and I may as well get my ticket's worth."

Meg and Robin regarded her with interest. Aunt Matilda and the Midway Plaisance, taken together, would be such a startling contrast that they must be interesting. And as she looked at John Holt's face, as they went on

"IT'S A QUEER SIGHT," SHE SAID TO JOHN HOLT.

their way, Meg knew he was thinking the same thing.
And it was a strange experience. Mrs. Jennings strode
through the curious places rather as if she were following
a plough down a furrow. She looked at Samoan beauties,
Arab chiefs, and Persian Jersey Lilies with unmovedly
scrutinizing eyes. She did not waste time anywhere, but
she took all in as if it were a matter of business. Camel
drivers and donkey boys seemed to strike her merely as
samples of slow travelling; she ascended, as it were into
mid-heaven, on the Ferris Wheel, with a grim air of determination. Being so lifted from earth and poised above in
the clear air, Meg had thrilled with a strange, exultant
feeling of being a bird, and it had seemed to her that, with
a moment's flutter of wings, she could soar higher and
higher, and lose herself in the pure sea of blue above.
Aunt Matilda looked down with cool interest.

"Pretty big power this," she said to John Holt. "I
guess it's made one man's fortune."

John Holt was a generous host. He took her from
place to place—to Lapland villages, Cannibal huts, and
Moorish palaces. She tramped about, and inspected them
all with a sharp, unenthusiastic eye. She looked at the men
and women, and their strange costumes, plainly thinking
them rather mad.

"It's a queer sight," she said to John Holt; "but I
don't see what good all this is going to do any one."

"It saves travelling expenses," answered John Holt,

laughing.   His shrewd, humorous face was very full of
expression all the time they were walking about together.
She had only come for the day, and she was going back by
a night train.   When she left them, she gave them both
one of those newly appreciative looks.

"Well," she said, "Mr. Holt's going to look after you,
he says.   He's got something to tell you when I'm gone.
We've talked it over, and it's all right.   There's one thing
sure, you're two of the luckiest young ones *I*'ve heard
of."   And she marched away briskly.

Meg and Robin looked at each other and at John Holt.
What was he going to tell them?   But he told them
nothing until they had all dined, and Ben and his mother
had gone home, prepared to come again the next day.

By that time the City Beautiful was wreathed with its
enchanted jewels of light again, and in the lagoon's depths
they trembled and blazed.   John Holt called a gondola
with a brilliant gondolier, and they got into it and shot out
into the radiant night.

The sight was so unearthly in its beauty that for a few
moments they were quite still.   Meg sat in her Straw
Parlor attitude, with her elbows on her knees, and her chin
on her hands.   Her eyes looked very big, and as lustrous
as the jewels in the lagoon.

"I'm going to ask you something," said John Holt, in a
quiet sort of voice, at last.

"Yes," said Meg, dreamily.

"Would you two like to belong to *me*?"

Meg's hands dropped, and she turned her shining eyes.

"I've been talking to your Aunt Matilda about that big house of mine," he went on. "It's empty. There's too much room in it. I want to take you two, and see if you can fill it up. Will you come?"

Meg and Robin turned their eyes upon each other in a dazed way.

"Will we come?" they stammered.

"Mrs. Jennings is willing," said John Holt. "You two have things to do in the world. I'll help you to learn to do them. You," with the short laugh—"you shall tell me fairy stories."

Fairy stories! What was this? Their hearts beat in their breasts like little hammers. The gondola moved smoothly over the scintillating water, and the jewel-strung towers and domes rose white against the lovely night. Meg looked around her, and uttered a little cry.

"Oh, Rob!" she said. "Oh, dear John Holt. We have got *into* the City Beautiful, and you are going to let us live there always."

And John Holt knew that the big house would seem empty no more.

XX

IT would have seemed that this was the climax of wonders and delights—to know that they had escaped forever from Aunt Matilda's world, that they were not to be parted from John Holt, that they were to be like his children, living with him, sharing his great house, and learning all they could want to learn. All this, even when it was spoken of as possible, seemed more than could be believed, but it seemed almost more unbelievable day by day, as the truth began to realize itself in detail. What a marvellous thing it was to find out that they were not lonely, uncared-for creatures any more, but that they belonged to a man who seemed to hold all power in his hands! When John Holt took them to the big stores and bought them all they needed, new clothes and new trunks and new comforts, and luxuries such as they had never thought of as belonging to them, they felt almost aghast. He was so practical, and seemed to know so well how to do everything, that each hour convinced them more and more that everything was possible to him. And he seemed to like so much to be with them. Day after day he took them to their City Beautiful, and enjoyed with them every treasure in it. And they had so much time before them, they could see it all at rapturous

leisure and ease.   No more hungry hours, no more straining
of tired bodies and spurring of weary feet, because there
was so much to see and so little time to see it in, because
there was so little money to be spent.   There was time to
loiter through palaces and linger before pictures and marvellous things.   And John Holt could explain them all.
No more limited and vague imaginings.   There was time to
hear everything, and Meg could tell fairy stories by the hour
if she was in the mood.   She told them in tropical bowers;
she told them as they floated on the lagoon; she read them
in strange, savage, or oriental faces.

"I shall have enough to last all my life, John Holt,"
she would say.   "I see a new one every half-hour.   If you
like, I will tell them all to you and Robin when you have
nothing else to do."

"It will be like the 'Arabian Nights,'" said Robin.
"Meg, do you remember that old book we had, where all
the leaves we wanted most were torn out, and we had to
make the rest up ourselves?"

There was one story Meg found John Holt liked better
than all the rest.   It was the one about the City Beautiful,
into which she used to follow Christian in the days when
she and Robin lay in the Straw Parlor.   It had grown so
real to her that she made it very real and near in the telling.
John Holt liked the way she had of filling it with people
and things she knew quite well.   Meg was very simple
about it all, but she told that story well and often, when

they were resting in some beautiful place alone.   John Holt
would lead her back to it, and sit beside her, listening, with
a singular expression in his eyes.   Ah, those were wonderful days !

Ben and his mother shared them, though they were not
always with John Holt and Robin and Meg. John Holt
made comfortable plans for them, and let them wander about
and look their fill.

"It's a great thing for *him*, Mr. Holt," said the poor
woman once, with a side glance at Ben. "Seems like he's
been born over again. The way he talks, when we go home
at night, is as if he'd never be tired again as long as he lives.
And a month ago I used to think he'd wear himself out,
fretting. Seemed like I could see him getting thinner and
peakeder every day. My, it's a wonderful thing !"

And John Holt's kindness did not end there, though it
was some time before Meg and Robin heard all he had
done. One day, when they had left the grounds earlier
than usual, because they were tired, he spent the evening in
searching out Ben's disreputable father, and giving him what
he called "a straight talk."

"Look here," he said, "I'm going to keep my eye on
that boy of yours and your wife. I intend to make the
house decent, and see that the boy has a chance to learn
something, and take care they're not too hard run. But I'm
going to keep my eye on you too—at least, I shall see that
some one else does—and if you make things uncomfortable

you'll be made pretty uncomfortable yourself, that's all. I'd advise you to try the new recreation of going to work. It'll be good for your health. Sort of athletics."

And he kept his word.

It was a marvel of a holiday. It is not possible that among all the holiday-makers there were two others who were nearer the rapture of Paradise than these two little Pilgrims.

When it was at an end they went home with John Holt. It was a wonderful home-going. The house was a wonderful house. It was one of the remarkable places that some self-made western men have built and furnished, with the aid of unlimited fortunes and the unlimited shrewd good sense which has taught most of those of them whose lives have been spent in work and bold ventures that it is more practical to buy taste and experience than to spend money without it. John Holt had also had the aid and taste of a wonderful little woman, whose life had been easier and whose world had been broader than his own. Together they had built a beautiful and lovable home to live in. It contained things from many countries, and its charm and luxury might well have been the result of a far older civilization.

"Don't you think, Robin," said Meg, in a low voice, the first evening, as they sat in a deep-cushioned window-seat in the library together, "don't you think you know what She was like?"

They had spoken together of her often, and somehow it was always in a rather low voice, and they always called her " She."

Robin looked up from the book he held on his knee. It was a beautiful volume She had been fond of.

" I know why you say that," he said. " You mean that somehow the house is like her. Yes, I'm sure it is, just as Aunt Matilda's house is like her. People's houses are always like them."

" This one is full of her," said Meg. " I should think John Holt would feel as if she must be in it, and she might speak to him any moment. I feel as if she might speak to me. And it isn't only the pictures of her everywhere, with her eyes laughing at you from the wall and the tables and the mantels. It's *herself.* Perhaps it is because she helped John Holt to choose things, and was so happy here."

" Perhaps it is," said Robin ; and he added, softly, " this was her book."

They went once more to Aunt Matilda's world. They did it because John Holt wanted to see the Straw Parlor, and they wanted to show it to him and bid it good-by.

Aunt Matilda treated them with curious consideration. It almost seemed as if she had begun to regard them with respect. It seemed to her that any business-like person would respect two penniless children who had made themselves attractive to a man with the biggest farm in Illinois,

and other resources still larger. They went out to the
barn in their old way, when no one knew where they
were going, and when no one was about to see them place
their ladder against the stack, and climb up to the top.
The roof seemed more like a dark tent than ever, and
they saw the old birds' nests, which by this time were
empty.

"Meg," said Robin, "do you remember the day we
lay in the straw and told each other we had got work?
And do you remember the afternoon I climbed up with
the old coffee-pot, to boil the eggs in?"

"And when we counted the Treasure?" said Meg.

"And when we talked about miracles?" said Robin.

"And when it made me think human beings could
do anything if they tried hard enough?" said Meg.

"And when you read the 'Pilgrim's Progress'?" said
John Holt.

"And the first afternoon when we listened to Jones
and Jerry, and you said there *was* a City Beautiful?" said
Meg.

"And there *was*," said Robin, "and we've been there."

"It was just this time in the afternoon," said Meg,
looking about her; "the red light was dying away, for I
could not see to read any more."

And for a little while they sat in the Straw Parlor,
while the red light waned; and afterwards, when they spoke
of it, they found they were all thinking of the same thing,

and it was of the last day they had spent at the Enchanted
City, when they had gone about together in a strange,
tender, half-sad mood, loitering through the white palaces,
lingering about the clear pools of green sea water, where
strange creatures swam lazily or darted to and fro, looking their last at pictures and stories in marble, and listening to the tinkle of water plashing under great tropical
leaves and over strange mosses, strolling through temples
and past savage huts, and gazing in final questioning at
mysterious, barbarous faces; and at last passing through
the stately archway and being borne away on the waters
of the great lake.

As they had been carried away farther and farther, and
the white wonder had begun to lose itself and fade into
a white spirit of a strange and lovely thing, Meg had felt
the familiar throb at her heart and the familiar lump in
her throat.   And she had broken into a piteous little
cry.

"Oh, John Holt," she said, "it is going, it is going,
and we shall never see it again! For it will vanish away,
it will vanish away!" And the tears rushed down her
cheeks, and she hid her face on his arm.

But though he had laughed his short laugh, John
Holt had made her lift up her head.

"No," he said, "it won't vanish away. It's not one of
the things that vanish. Things don't vanish away that
a million or so of people have seen as they've seen this.

They stay where they're not forgotten, and time doesn't change them. They're put where they can be passed on, and passed on again. And thoughts that grow out of them bring other ones. And what things may grow out of it that never would have been, and where the end is, the Lord only knows, for no human being can tell. It won't vanish away."

Perhaps, as Meg said often to John Holt, theirs was a fairy story—and why not? There are beautiful things in the world, there are men and women and children with brave and gentle hearts; there are those who work well and give to others the thing they have to give, and are glad in the giving. There are birds in the sky and flowers in the woods, and Spring comes every year. And these are the fairy stories.

CHARLES SCRIBNER'S SONS'

New and Standard Books for Young Readers
for 1895=96.

A New Book by Mrs. Burnett.

TWO LITTLE PILGRIMS' PROGRESS:

A Story of the City Beautiful. By Mrs. FRANCES
HODGSON BURNETT. Illustrated by R. B. BIRCH.
Uniform with "Fauntleroy," etc. Sq. 8vo, $1.50.

The largest and most notable children's book that Mrs.
Burnett has written since "Fauntleroy." It is a charming story
of a little boy and girl, who, taking their small savings, leave
home to visit the World's Fair. This is their Pilgrims' Progress;
and their interesting adventures and the happy ending of it all
Mrs. Burnett tells as no one else can. It is in the author's best
vein and will take place in the hearts of her readers close beside
"Fauntleroy."

Mrs. Burnett's Five Famous Juveniles.

LITTLE LORD FAUNTLEROY.

Beautifully illustrated by REGINALD B. BIRCH. Square 8vo, $2.00.

" In 'Little Lord Fauntleroy' we gain another charming child to add to our gallery of juvenile heroes and heroines ; one
who teaches a great lesson with such truth and sweetness that we part from him with real regret."—LOUISA M. ALCOTT.

SARA CREWE;

Or, What happened at Miss Minchin's. Richly and fully illustrated by R. B. BIRCH. Square 8vo, $1.00.

" It is a story to linger over in the reading, it is so brightly, frankly, sweetly, and tenderly
written, and to remember and return to. In creating her little gentlewoman, 'Sara Crewe,' so fresh,
so simple, so natural, so genuine, and so indomitable, Mrs. Burnett has added another child to
English Fiction."—R. H. STODDARD.

LITTLE SAINT ELIZABETH

And Other Stories. With twelve full-page drawings by
REGINALD B. BIRCH. Square 8vo, $1.50.

" Four stories different in kind, but alike in grace and spirit."—SUSAN COOLIDGE.
" One of the most winning and pathetic of Mrs. Burnett's child heroines. The tales which follov
are quite charming."—THE ATHENÆUM.

GIOVANNI AND THE OTHER:

Children who have made stories. With nine full-page illustrations by REGINALD B. BIRCH. Square 8vo, $1.50.

" Stories beautiful in tone, and style, and color."—KATE DOUGLAS WIGGIN.

" There is a tender pathos in these tales and a gentle, loving spirit that gives the book a peculiar
charm."—PHILADELPHIA TIMES.

PICCINO

And Other Child Stories. Fully illustrated by R. B. BIRCH.
Square 8vo, $1.50.

" The history of Piccino's 'two days' is as delicate as one of the anemones that spring in the
rock walls facing Piccino's Mediterranean. . . . The other stories in the book have the charm of
their predecessor in material and matter."—MRS. BURTON HARRISON.

Charles Scribner's Sons' Books for Young Readers.

Written and Illustrated by Howard Pyle.

A NEW BOOK JUST PUBLISHED.

BEHIND THE GARDEN OF THE MOON.

A Real Story of the Moon Angel. Written and illustrated by HOWARD PYLE. Square 12mo, $2.00.

Underneath the charm of this original and delightful fairy tale of Mr. Pyle's is a mystical moral significance which gives it the dignity of true literature in addition to its interest of adventure. Out of the truth that great deeds are achieved and high character moulded by entire spiritual consecration, rather than by direct and interested effort, the author has evolved a winning and delightful piece of fanciful fiction, and has illustrated it copiously in his happiest and most characteristically poetical vein.

OTHER BOOKS BY MR. PYLE.

THE MERRY ADVENTURES OF ROBIN HOOD

of Great Renown in Nottinghamshire. With many illustrations. Royal 8vo, $3.00.

"This superb book is unquestionably the most original and elaborate ever produced by any American artist. Mr. Pyle has told, with pencil and pen, the complete and consecutive story of Robin Hood and his merry men their haunts in Sherwood Forest, gathered from the old ballads and legends. Mr. Pyle's admirable illustrations are strewn profusely through the book."— BOSTON TRANSCRIPT.

OTTO OF THE SILVER HAND.

With many illustrations. Royal 8vo, half leather, $2.00.

"The scene of the story is mediæval Germany in the time of the feuds and robber barons and romance. The kidnapping of Otto, his adventures among rough soldiers, and his daring rescue, make up a spirited and thrilling story. The drawings are in keeping with the text, and in mechanical and artistic qualities as well as in literary execution the book must be greeted as one of the very best juveniles of the year, quite worthy to succeed to the remarkable popularity of Mr. Pyle's 'Robin Hood.'"—CHRISTIAN UNION.

FROM "OTTO OF THE SILVER HAND."
Reduced.

Charles Scribner's Sons' Books for Young Readers.

The Kanter Girls.

By Mary L. B. BRANCH. Illustrated by Helen M. Armstrong.
Square 12mo, $1.50.

The adventures of Janet and Prue, two small sisters, among different peoples of the imaginative world—dryads, snow-children, Kobolds, &c.—aided by their invisible rings, their magic boat, and their wonderful birds, are described by the author with great naturalness and a true gift for story-telling. The numerous illustrations are very attractive and in thorough sympathy with the text.

A New Book by Gordon Stables.

FOR LIFE AND LIBERTY.

A Story of Battle by Land and Sea. By GORDON STABLES. With 8 full-page illustrations. 12mo, $1.50.

The story of an English boy who runs from home and joins the southern army in the late civil war. He is accompanied by his chum, who enters the navy, and their various adventures in the great conflict are set forth with great vigor and are unfailing in interest.

OTHER BOOKS BY MR. STABLES.

TO GREENLAND AND THE POLE.

A Story of Adventure in the Arctic Regions. With 8 full-page illustrations. 12mo, $1.50.

" More than ordinarily entertaining and it imparts agreeably a great deal of valuable knowledge."—CONGREGATIONALIST.

WESTWARD WITH COLUMBUS.

Illustrated. 12mo, 1.50.

" The whole story of Columbus' career is embraced, but the main interest is focused on the westward voyage and the romantic incidents of the discovery. The book is admirably written and is well illustrated."—BOSTON BEACON.

'TWIXT SCHOOL AND COLLEGE.

A Tale of Self-Reliance. With 8 illustrations. Crown 8vo, $1.50.

Joseph The Dreamer.

By the Author of Jesus the Carpenter. 12mo, in press.

The story of Joseph, told in the same popular, interesting, and realistic manner as that of Jesus in the author's former book; not only setting forth truthfully and graphically the life of Joseph, but picturing as well the marvellous state of Egypt in which he lived.

JESUS THE CARPENTER. By A. LAYMAN. 12mo, $1.50.

" I think the idea of this book—the aim and the intention—excellent, and the execution beautiful."—PROF. A. B. BRUCE.

A New Book by Kirk Munroe.

AT WAR WITH PONTIAC;

Or, The Totem of the Bear.   A Tale of Redcoat and Redskin.
By KIRK MUNROE.   With 8 full-page illustrations by J.
FINNEMORE. 12mo, $1.25.

A story of old days in America when Detroit was a frontier town and
the shores of Lake Erie were held by hostile Indians under Pontiac. The
hero, Donald Hester, goes in search of his sister Edith, who has been captured by the Indians. Strange and terrible are his experiences : for he is
wounded, taken prisoner, condemned to be burned, and contrives to escape.
In the end there is peace between Pontiac and the English, and all things
terminate happily for the hero.   One dares not skip a page of this enthralling
story.

THE WHITE CONQUEROR.

A Tale of Toltec and Aztec.   By KIRK MUNROE.   With 8
full-page illustrations by W. S. STACEY.   12mo, $1.25.

"The story is replete with scenes of vivid power; it is full of action and rapid movement; and he must be deficient in recep-
tive faculty who fails to gain valuable historical instruction, along with the pleasure of reading a tale graphically told."—PHILA-
DELPHIA BULLETIN.

Stories of Literature, Science, and History.

By HENRIETTA CHRISTIAN WRIGHT.

A NEW VOLUME JUST ISSUED.

CHILDREN'S STORIES IN AMERICAN LITERATURE—1660-1860.   12mo, $1.25.

Miss Wright here continues her attractive presentation of literary history begun in her "Children's Stories in English Literature."   Elliot, the translator of the Bible into the English language,
Irving, Cooper, Prescott, Holmes, Longfellow, Hawthorne, Mrs. Stowe, Whittier, Poe, and Emer-
son are here considered, bringing the history of the subject down to the period of the civil war, and
treated with constant reference to that side of their works and personalities which most nearly ap-
peals to children.

CHILDREN'S STORIES IN ENGLISH LITERATURE.   Two volumes :
TALIESIN TO SHAKESPEARE—SHAKESPEARE TO TENNYSON. 12mo, each, $1.25.

"It is indeed a vivid history of the people as well as a story of their literature; and, brief as it is,
the author has so deftly seized on all the salient points, that the child who has read this book will be
more thoroughly acquainted than many a student of history with the life and thought of the centuries over which the work reaches."—THE EVANGELIST.

CHILDREN'S STORIES OF THE GREAT SCIENTISTS.   With portraits.
12mo, $1.25.

"The author has succeeded in making her pen-pictures of the great scientists as graphic as the
excellent portraits that illustrate the work.   Around each name she has picturesquely grouped the
essential features of scientific achievement."—BROOKLYN TIMES.

CHILDREN'S STORIES IN AMERICAN HISTORY.   Illustrated.   12mo,
$1.25.

"A most delightful and instructive collection of historical events, told in a simple and pleasant
manner.   Almost every occurrence in the gradual development of our country is woven into an
attractive story."—SAN FRANCISCO EVENING POST.

CHILDREN'S STORIES OF AMERICAN PROGRESS.   Illustrated.   12mo, $1.25.

"Miss Wright is favorably known by her volume of well-told 'Stories in American History;' and her 'Stories of American
Progress' is equally worthy of commendation.   Taken together they present a series of pictures of great graphic interest.
The illustrations are excellent."—THE NATION.

G. A. Henty's Popular Stories for Boys.

NEW VOLUMES FOR 1895-96.

Each, Crown 8vo. Handsomely Illustrated. $1.50.

Mr. Henty, the most popular writer of Books of Adventure in England, adds three new volumes to his list this fall—books that will delight the thousands of boys who are his ardent admirers.

"Mr. Henty's books never fail to interest boy readers. Among writers of stories of adventure he stands in the very first rank."—ACADEMY (London).

"No country nor epoch of history is there which Mr. Henty does not know, and what is really remarkable is that he always writes well and interestingly. Boys like stirring adventures, and Mr. Henty is a master of this method of composition."—NEW YORK TIMES.

A KNIGHT OF THE WHITE CROSS.

A Tale of the Siege of Rhodes. With 12 full-page illustrations.

G. A. HENTY.

Gervaise Tresham, the hero of this story, joins the Order of the Knights of St. John, and leaving England he proceeds to the stronghold of Rhodes. Subsequently, Gervaise is made a Knight of the White Cross for valor, while soon after he is appointed commander of a war-galley, and in his first voyage destroys a fleet of Moorish corsairs. During one of his cruises the young knight is attacked on shore, captured after a desperate struggle, and sold into slavery in Tripoli. He succeeds in escaping, however, and returns to Rhodes in time to take part in the splendid defence of that fortress. Altogether a fine chivalrous tale, of varied interest and full of noble daring.

THE TIGER OF MYSORE.

A Story of the War with Tippoo Saib. With 12 full-page illustrations.

Dick Holland, whose father is supposed to be a captive of Tippoo Saib, goes to India to help him to escape. He joins the army under Lord Cornwallis, and takes part in the campaign against Tippoo. Afterwards, he assumes a disguise, enters Seringapatam, the capital of Mysore, rescues Tippoo's harem from a tiger, and is appointed to high office by the tyrant. In this capacity Dick visits the hill fortresses, still in search of his father; and at last he discovers him in the great stronghold of Savandroog. The hazardous rescue through the enemy's country is at length accomplished, and the young fellow's dangerous mission is done.

A KNIGHT OF THE WHITE CROSS.

THROUGH RUSSIAN SNOWS.

A Story of Napoleon's Retreat from Moscow. With 8 full-page illustrations and a map.

The hero, Julian Wyatt, after several adventures with smugglers, by whom he is handed over a prisoner to the French, regains his freedom and joins Napoleon's army in the Russian campaign, and reaches Moscow with the victorious Emperor. Then, when the terrible retreat begins, Julian finds himself in the rear guard of the French army, fighting desperately, league by league, against famine, snow-storms, wolves, and Russians. Ultimately he escapes out of the general disaster, after rescuing the daughter of a Russian Count; makes his way to St. Petersburg, and then returns to England. A story with an excellent plot, exciting adventures, and splendid historical interests.

Charles Scribner's Sons' Books for Young Readers.

G. A. HENTY'S POPULAR STORIES FOR BOYS.

Each, Crown 8vo, handsomely illustrated, $1.50.

IN THE HEART OF THE ROCKIES. A STORY OF ADVENTURE IN COLORADO.

"One of the most interesting and attractive stories for boys. It is a tale of adventure thrilling enough for the most daring readers."—BOSTON JOURNAL.

WULF THE SAXON. A STORY OF THE NORMAN CONQUEST.

"An unusually realistic picture of the times. The scenes and incidents which Mr. Henty introduces are calculated to awaken fresh interest in the influence of the battle of Hastings upon the destiny of mankind."—BOSTON HERALD.

WHEN LONDON BURNED. A STORY OF RESTORATION TIMES AND THE GREAT FIRE.

"An exciting story of adventure, at the same time dealing with historic truths deftly and interestingly."—DETROIT FREE PRESS.

ST. BARTHOLOMEW'S EVE. A TALE OF THE HUGUENOT WARS.

"Exciting enough to interest even the dullest of readers."—BOSTON TRANSCRIPT.

THROUGH THE SIKH WAR. A TALE OF THE CONQUEST OF THE PUNJAUB.

"Not only interesting but instructive. It is related with great spirit and animation."—BOSTON HERALD.

A JACOBITE EXILE. BEING THE ADVENTURES OF A YOUNG ENGLISHMAN IN THE SERVICE OF CHARLES XII. OF SWEDEN.

"Remarkable for its thrilling adventures and its interesting historical pictures."—HERALD AND PRESBYTER.

BERIC THE BRITON. A STORY OF THE ROMAN INVASION.

"It is a powerful and fascinating romance."—BOSTON POST.

IN GREEK WATERS. A STORY OF THE GRECIAN WAR OF INDEPENDENCE—1821–1827.

"It is a stirring narrative, wholesome and stimulating."—CONGREGATIONALIST.

CONDEMNED AS A NIHILIST. A STORY OF ESCAPE FROM SIBERIA.

"A narrative absorbing and thrilling. The scenes of Siberian prison-life give the book a peculiar value."—CHRISTIAN ADVOCATE.

REDSKIN AND COWBOY. A TALE OF THE WESTERN PLAINS.

"Though it is full of hairbreadth escapes, none of the incidents are improbable. It is needless to say that the adventures are well told."—SAN FRANCISCO CHRONICLE.

HELD FAST FOR ENGLAND. A TALE OF THE SIEGE OF GIBRALTAR.

"It is an historical novel, the siege of Gibraltar, in the latter part of the eighteenth century, being the foundation on which Mr. Henty's clever action rests."—NEWARK ADVERTISER.

** *The above are Mr. Henty's latest books. A full descriptive list containing all of Mr. Henty's books — now 47 in number — will be sent to any address on application. They are all attractively illustrated and handsomely bound.*

Czar and Sultan.

The adventures of a British Lad in the Russo-Turkish War of 1877–78. By ARCHIBALD FORBES. Illustrated. 12mo, $2.00.

"Very fascinating and graphic. Mr. Forbes is a forcible writer, and the present work has the vigor and intensity associated with his name. It is sure to be popular with youthful readers."—BOSTON BEACON.

"A brilliant and exciting narrative, and the drawings add to its interest and value."—N. Y. OBSERVER.

Books of Adventure by Robert Leighton.

OLAF THE GLORIOUS.

A Story of Olaf Triggvison, King of Norway, A. D. 995–1000. Crown 8vo, with numerous full-page illustrations, $1.50.

THE WRECK OF THE GOLDEN FLEECE.

The Story of a North Sea Fisher Boy. Illustrated. Crown 8vo, $1.50.

THE THIRSTY SWORD.

A Story of the Norse Invasion of Scotland, 1262–65. With 8 illustrations and a map. Crown 8vo, $1.50.

THE PILOTS OF POMONA.

A Story of the Orkney Islands. With 8 illustrations and a map. Crown 8vo, $1.50.

"Mr. Leighton as a writer for boys needs no praise, as his books place him in the front rank."—NEW YORK OBSERVER.

Things Will Take a Turn.

By BEATRICE HARRADEN, author of "Ships that Pass in the Night." Illustrated. 12mo, $1.00.

The charm of this tale is its delicate, wistful sympathy. It is the story of a sunny-hearted child, Rosebud, who assists her grandfather in his dusty, second-hand bookshop. One cannot help being fascinated by the sweet little heroine, she is so engaging, so natural; and to love Rosebud is to love all her friends and enter sympathetically into the good fortune she brought them.

Among the Lawmakers.

By EDMUND ALTON. Illustrated. Sq. 8vo, $1.50.

"The book is a diverting as well as an instructive one. Mr. Alton was in his early days a page in the Senate, and he relates the doings of Congress from the point of view he then obtained. His narrative is easy and piquant, and abounds in personal anecdotes about the great men whom the pages waited on."—CHRISTIAN UNION.

Samuel Adams Drake's Historical Books.

THE MAKING OF THE OHIO VALLEY STATES. 1660–1837. Illustrated. 12mo, $1.50.

THE MAKING OF VIRGINIA AND THE MIDDLE COLONIES. 1578–1701. Illustrated. 12mo, $1.50.

THE MAKING OF NEW ENGLAND. 1580–1643. With 148 illustrations and with maps. 12mo, $1.50.

THE MAKING OF THE GREAT WEST. 1812–1853. With 145 illustrations and with maps. 12mo, $1.50.

"The author's aim in these books is that they shall occupy a place between the larger and lesser histories of the lands and of the periods of which they treat, and that each topic therein shall be treated as a unit and worked out to a clear understanding of its objects and results before passing to another topic. In the furtherance of this method each subject has its own descriptive notes, maps, plans and illustrations, the whole contributing to a thorough, though condensed, knowledge of the subject in hand."—NEW YORK MAIL AND EXPRESS.

The Butterfly Hunters in the Caribbees.

By Dr. EUGENE MURRAY-AARON. With 8 full-page illustrations. Square 12mo, $2.00.

"The book is written in a very interesting style. The author is a recognized authority on the subjects of which he writes. He takes a company of young explorers over ground with which he is thoroughly familiar."—THE INDEPENDENT.

"Our author only reproduces the incidents and scenes of his own life as an exploring naturalist in a way to capture the attention of younger readers. The incidents are told entertainingly, and his descriptions of country and the methods of capture of butterflies and bugs of rare varieties are full of interest."—CHICAGO INTER-OCEAN.

A New Mexico David.

AND OTHER STORIES AND SKETCHES OF THE SOUTH WEST. By CHARLES F. LUMMIS. Illustrated. 12mo, $1.25.

"Mr. Lummis has lived for years in the land of the Pueblos ; has traversed it in every direction, both on foot and on horseback ; and it is an enthralling treat set before youthful readers by him in this series of lively chronicles."—BOSTON BEACON.

EUGENE FIELD.

Poems of Childhood by Eugene Field.

LOVE SONGS OF CHILDHOOD. 16mo, $1.00.

WITH TRUMPET AND DRUM. By EUGENE FIELD. 16mo, $1.25.

"His poems of childhood have gone home, not only to the hearts of children, but to the heart of the country as well, and he is one of the few contributors to that genuine literature of childhood which expresses ideas from the standpoint of a child."—THE OUTLOOK.

Charles Scribner's Sons' Books for Young Readers.

The Wagner Story Book.

Firelight Tales of the Great Music Dramas.   By WILLIAM HENRY FROST.
Illustrated by SIDNEY R. BURLEIGH.   12mo, $1.50.

"A successful attempt to make the romantic themes of the music dramas intelligible to young readers. The author has full command of his subject, and the style is easy, graceful and simple."—BOSTON BEACON.

RICHARD WAGNER.

Robert Grant's Two Books for Boys.

JACK HALL: OR, THE SCHOOL DAYS OF AN AMERI-
CAN BOY.   Illustrated by F. G. ATTWOOD.
12mo, $1.25.

"A better book for boys has never been written. It is pure, clean and healthy, and has throughout a vigorous action that holds the reader breathlessly."—BOSTON HERALD.

"A capital story for boys, wholesome and interesting. It reminds one of Tom Brown."—BOSTON TRANSCRIPT.

JACK IN THE BUSH: OR, A SUMMER ON A SAL-
MON RIVER.   Illustrated by F. T. MERRILL.
12mo, $1.25.

"A clever book for boys. It is the story of the camp life of a lot of boys, and is destined to please every boy reader. It is attractively illustrated."—DETROIT FREE PRESS.

"An ideal story of out-door life and genuine experiences." —BOSTON TRAVELLER.

Illustrated Library of Travel.

By BAYARD TAYLOR.

Per set, six volumes, 12mo, $6.00.   Each with many illustrations.   Sold separately, per volume, $1.25.

JAPAN IN OUR DAY.
TRAVELS IN ARABIA.
TRAVELS IN SOUTH AFRICA.
CENTRAL ASIA.
THE LAKE REGION OF CENTRAL
    AFRICA.
SIAM, THE LAND OF THE WHITE
    ELEPHANT.

Each volume is complete in itself, and contains, first, a brief preliminary sketch of the country to which it is devoted; next, such an outline of previous explorations as may be necessary to explain what has been achieved by later ones; and finally, a condensation of one or more of the most important narratives of recent travel, accompanied with illustrations of the scenery, architecture, and life of the races, drawn only from the most authentic sources.

"Authenticated accounts of countries, peoples, modes of living and being, curiosities in natural history, and personal adventure in travels and explorations, suggest a rich fund of solid instruction combined with delightful entertainment. The editorship, by one of the most observant and well-traveled men of modern times, at once secures the high character of the 'Library' in every particular."—THE SUNDAY SCHOOL TIMES.

The Norseland Series.

BY H. H. BOYESEN.

NORSELAND TALES. Illustrated. 12mo, $1.25.

BOYHOOD IN NORWAY : Nine Stories of Deeds of the Sons of the Vikings. With 8 illustrations. 12mo, $1.25

AGAINST HEAVY ODDS, and a Fearless Trio. With 13 full-page illustrations by W. L. Taylor. 12mo, $1.25.

THE MODERN VIKINGS : Stories of Life and Sport in the Norseland. With many full-page illustrations. 12mo, $1.25.

The four above volumes in a box, $5.00.

" Charmingly told stories of boy-life in the Land of the Midnight Sun, illustrated with pictures giving a capital idea of the incidents and scenes described. The tales have a delight all their own, as they tell of scenes and sports and circumstances so different from those of our American life."—N. Y. Observer.

Two Books by Rossiter Johnson.

THE END OF A RAINBOW. An American Story. Illustrated. 12mo, $1.50.

" It will be read with breathless interest. It is interesting and full of boyish experiences."— N. Y. Independent.

PHAETON ROGERS. A Novel of Boy Life. Illustrated. 12mo, $1.50.

" Mr. Johnson has shown in this book capabilities of a really high quality, for his story abounds with humor, and there are endless bits of quiet fun in it, which bring out the hearty laugh, even when it is read by older people. It is a capital book for boys."—New York Times.

Mrs. Burton Harrison's Tales.

BRIC-A-BRAC STORIES.

With 24 illustrations by Walter Crane. 12mo, $1.50.

" When the little boy, for whose benefit the various articles of bric-a-brac in his father's drawing-room relate stories appropriate to their several native countries, exclaims at the conclusion of one of them : ' I almost think there can't be a better one than that !' the reader, of whatever age, will probably feel inclined to agree with him. Upon the whole, it is to be wished that every boy and girl might become acquainted with the contents of this book."—Julian Hawthorne.

THE OLD FASHIONED FAIRY BOOK.

Illustrated by Rosina Emmet. 16mo, $1.25.

" The little ones, who so willingly go back with us to 'Jack the Giant Killer,' 'Bluebeard,' and the kindred stories of our childhood, will gladly welcome Mrs. Burton Harrison's 'Old-Fashioned Fairy Tales.' The graceful pencil of Miss Rosina Emmet has given a pictorial interest to the book."—Frank R. Stockton.

FROM " BRIC-A-BRAC STORIES."
Reduced.

Charles Scribner's Sons' Books for Young Readers.

Frank R. Stockton's Books for the Young.

"His books for boys and girls are classics."—Newark Advertiser.

THE CLOCKS OF RONDAINE, and Other Stories. With 24 illustrations by Blashfield, Rogers, Beard, and others. Square 8vo, $1.50.

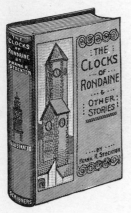

PERSONALLY CONDUCTED. Illustrated by Pennell, Parsons, and others. Sq. 8vo, $2.00.

THE STORY OF VITEAU. Illustrated by R. B. Birch. 12mo, $1.50.

A JOLLY FELLOWSHIP. With 20 illustrations. 12mo, $1.50.

THE FLOATING PRINCE AND OTHER FAIRY TALES. Illustrated. Square 8vo, $1.50.

THE TING-A-LING TALES. Illustrated. 12mo, $1.00.

FRANK R. STOCKTON.

ROUNDABOUT RAMBLES IN LANDS OF FACT AND FICTION. Illustrated. Square 8vo, $1.50.

TALES OUT OF SCHOOL. With nearly 200 illustrations. Square 8vo, $1.50.

"The volumes are profusely illustrated and contain the most entertaining sketches in Mr. Stockton's most entertaining manner."—Christian Union.

Edward Eggleston's Two Popular Books.

THE HOOSIER SCHOOL-BOY.	QUEER STORIES FOR BOYS AND

THE HOOSIER SCHOOL-BOY. Illustrated. 12mo, $1.00.

"'The Hoosier School-Boy' depicts some of the characteristics of boy-life years ago on the Ohio; characteristics, however, that were not peculiar to that section. The story presents a vivid and interesting picture of the difficulties which in those days beset the path of the youth aspiring for an education."—Chicago Inter-Ocean.

QUEER STORIES FOR BOYS AND GIRLS. 12mo, $1.00.

"A very bright and attractive little volume for young readers. The stories are fresh, breezy, and healthy, with a good point to them and a good, sound American view of life and the road to success. The book abounds in good feeling and good sense, and is written in a style of homely art."—Independent.

Evening Tales.

Done into English from the French of Frederic Ortoli, by Joel Chandler Harris. 12mo, $1.00.

"It is a veritable French 'Uncle Remus' that Mr. Harris has discovered in Frederic Ortoli. The book has the genuine piquancy of Gallic wit, and will be sure to charm American children. Mr. Harris's version is delightfully written."—Boston Beacon.

Hans Brinker:

Or, The Silver Skates. A Story of Life in Holland. By Mary Mapes Dodge. With 60 illustrations. 12mo, $1.50.

"The author has shown, in her former works for the young, a very rare ability to meet their wants; but she has produced nothing better than this charming tale—alive with incident and action, adorned rather than freighted with useful facts, and moral without moralization."—The Nation.

Thomas Nelson Page's Two Books.

AMONG THE CAMPS: OR, YOUNG PEOPLE'S STORIES OF THE WAR. With 8 full-page illustrations. Square, 8vo, $1.50.

"They are five in number, each having reference to some incident of the Civil War. A vein of mingled pathos and humor runs through them all, and greatly heightens the charm of them. It is the early experience of the author himself, doubtless, which makes his pictures of life in a Southern home during the great struggle so vivid and truthful."—THE NATION.

TWO LITTLE CONFEDERATES. With 8 full-page illustrations by KEMBLE and REDWOOD. Square, 8vo, $1.50.

"Mr. Page was 'raised' in Virginia, and he knows the 'darkey' of the South better than any one who writes about them. And he knows 'white folks,' too, and his stories, whether for old or young people, have the charm of sincerity and beauty and reality."—HARPER'S YOUNG PEOPLE.

W. O. Stoddard's Books for Boys.

DAB KINZER. A STORY OF A GROWING BOY. THE QUARTET. A SEQUEL TO DAB KINZER. SALTILLO BOYS. AMONG THE LAKES. WINTER FUN.

Five volumes, 12mo, in a box, $5.00. Sold separately, each, $1.00.

"William O. Stoddard has written capital books for boys. His 'Dab Kinzer' and 'The Quartet' are among the best specimens of 'Juveniles' produced anywhere. In his latest volume, 'Winter Fun,' Mr. Stoddard gives free rein to his remarkable gift of story-telling for boys. Healthful works of this kind cannot be too freely distributed among the little men of America." —NEW YORK JOURNAL OF COMMERCE.

Little People

And their Homes in Meadows, Woods, and Waters. By STELLA LOUISE HOOK. Illustrated by DAN BEARD and HARRY BEARD. One volume, square 8vo, $1.50.

"A delightful excursion for the little ones into the fairy-land of nature, telling all about the little people and all in such pleasant language and such pretty illustrations that the little readers will be charmed as much as they will be instructed by the book."—NEW YORK EVANGELIST.

Two Books by Robert Louis Stevenson.

THE BLACK ARROW:

A Tale of the Two Roses. By R. L. STEVENSON. With 12 full-page illustrations by WILL H. LOW and ALFRED BRENNAN. 12mo, $1.00.

"The story is one of the strongest pieces of romantic writing ever done by Mr. Stevenson." —THE BOSTON TIMES.

KIDNAPPED:

Being Memoirs of the Adventures of David Balfour in the Year 1751. By R. L. STEVENSON. 12mo, with 16 full-page illustrations, $1.00.

"Mr. Stevenson has never appeared to greater advantage than in 'Kidnapped.'"—THE NATION.

R. L. STEVENSON.

Kent Hampden.

A Story of a Boy. By REBECCA HARDING DAVIS. Illustrated by RUFUS F. ZOGBAUM. 12mo, $1.00.

Mrs. Davis's story of the heroic lad, who by his courage, faith, and persistency freed his father's good name from suspicion and overcame his enemies, is a valuable and entertaining study of life in West Virginia seventy years ago.

"Sharply drawn incidents and a crisp narrative make the book interesting."—BOSTON JOURNAL."

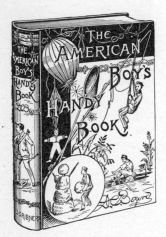

Two Books of Sports and Games.

THE AMERICAN BOY'S HANDY BOOK;

Or, What to Do and How to Do It. By DANIEL C. BEARD. With 360 illustrations by the author. Square 8vo, $2.00.

"The book has this great advantage over its predecessors, that most of the games, tricks, and other amusements described in it, are new. It treats of sports adapted to all seasons of the year; it is practical, and it is well illustrated."—NEW YORK TRIBUNE.

THE AMERICAN GIRL'S HANDY BOOK.

By LENA and ADELIA B. BEARD. With over 500 illustrations by the authors. Square 8vo, $2.00.

LOUISA M. ALCOTT: "I have put it in my list of good and useful books for young people, as I have many requests for advice from my little friends and their anxious mothers. I am most happy to commend your very ingenious and entertaining book."

The Boys' Library of Pluck and Action.

Illustrated. Four volumes, 12mo, in a box, $5.00. Sold separately, per volume, $1.50.

The purpose of "The Boy's Library of Pluck and Action" was to bring together the representative and most popular books of four of the best known writers for young people. Each of these books is fully described elsewhere in this catalogue. The volumes are beautifully illustrated and are uniformly bound.

THE BOY EMIGRANTS. By NOAH BROOKS.

PHAETON ROGERS. By ROSSITER JOHNSON.

A JOLLY FELLOWSHIP. By F. R. STOCKTON.

HANS BRINKER. By MRS. MARY M. DODGE.

Charles Scribner's Sons' Books for Young Readers.

Stories for Boys.

By RICHARD HARDING DAVIS.   With 6 full-page illustrations.   12mo, $1.00

CONTENTS : The Reporter who made himself King—Midsummer Pi-
rates—Richard Carr's Baby, a Football Story—The Great Tri-Club
Tennis Tournament—The Jump at Corey's Slip—The Van Bibber
Baseball Club—The Story of a Jockey.

"It will be astonishing indeed if youths of all ages are not fascinated with these
'Stories for Boys.' Mr. Davis knows infallibly what will interest his young readers."
—BOSTON BEACON.

RICHARD HARDING DAVIS.

Marvels of Animal Life Series.

FROM "THE IVORY KING."
Reduced.

By CHARLES F. HOLDER. Three volumes, 8vo,
each profusely illustrated.   Singly, $1.75;
the Set, $5.00.

THE IVORY KING. A POPULAR HISTORY OF THE ELE-
PHANT AND ITS ALLIES.

"The author talks in a lively and pleasant way about white
elephants, rogue elephants, baby elephants, trick elephants, of the
elephant in war, pageantry, sports and games. A charming accession
to books for young people."—CHICAGO INTERIOR.

MARVELS OF ANIMAL LIFE.

"Mr. Holder combines his description of these odd creatures with
stories of his own adventures in pursuit of them in many parts of the
world. These are told with much spirit, and add greatly to the fasci-
nation of the book."—WORCESTER SPY.

LIVING LIGHTS. A POPULAR ACCOUNT OF PHOSPHOR-
ESCENT ANIMALS AND VEGETABLES.

"A very curious branch of natural history is expounded in most
agreeable style by this delightful book. He has revealed a world of
new wonders."—PHILADELPHIA BULLETIN.

White Cockades.

An Incident of the "Forty-five."   By EDWARD I. STEVENSON.   12mo, $1.00.

"A bright historical tale. The scene is Scotland ; the time that of Prince Charles' rebellion. The hero is a certain gallant
young nobleman devoted to the last of the Stuarts and his cause. The action turns mainly upon the hiding, the hunting, and the
narrow escapes of Lord Geoffrey Armitage from the spies and soldiers of the King."—NEW YORK MAIL AND EXPRESS.

Prince Peerless.

A Fairy-Folk Story Book.   By MARGARET COLLIER (Madam Gelletti Di Cadilhac).
Illustrated by John Collier.   12mo, $1.25.

"More admirable and fascinating a fairy-story book we have not lately set eyes upon. The stories are most airily conceived
and gracefully executed."—HARTFORD POST.

Charles Scribner's Sons' Books for Young Readers.

Heroes of the Olden Time.

By JAMES BALDWIN.   Three volumes, 12mo, each
beautifully illustrated.   Singly, $1.50;
the set, $4.00.

A STORY OF THE GOLDEN AGE.   Illustrated
by HOWARD PYLE.

"Mr. Baldwin's book is redolent with the spirit of the Odyssey, that glorious primitive epic, fresh with the dew of the morning of time.   It is an unalloyed pleasure to read his recital of the adventures of the wily Odysseus.   Howard Pyle's illustrations render the spirit of the Homeric age with admirable felicity."—PROF. H. H. BOYESEN.

THE STORY OF SIEGFRIED.   Illustrated by HOWARD PYLE.

"The story of 'Siegfried' is charmingly told.   The author makes up the story from the various myths in a fascinating way which cannot fail to interest the reader.   It is as enjoyable as any fairy tale."—HARTFORD COURANT.

THE STORY OF ROLAND.   Illustrated by R. B. BIRCH.

"Mr. Baldwin has culled from a wide range of epics, French, Italian, and German, and has once more proved his aptitude as a story-teller for the young."—THE NATION.

The Boy's Library of Legend and Chivalry.

Edited by SIDNEY LANIER, and richly illustrated by FREDERICKS, BENSELL, and
KAPPES.   Four volumes, cloth, uniform binding, price per set, $7.00. Sold
separately, price per volume, $2.00.

Mr. Lanier's books present to boy readers the old English classics of history and legend in an attractive form.   While they are stories of action and stirring incident, they teach those lessons which manly, honest boys ought to learn.

THE BOY'S KING ARTHUR.

THE BOY'S FROISSART.

THE BOY'S PERCY.

THE KNIGHTLY LEGENDS OF
WALES.

"Amid all the strange and fanciful scenery of these stories, character and ideals of character remain at the simplest and purest.   The romantic history transpires in the healthy atmosphere of the open air on the green earth beneath the open sky."
—THE INDEPENDENT.

Charles Scribner's Sons' Books for Young Readers.

Two Books by Henry M. Stanley.

MY DARK COMPANIONS

And Their Strange Stories. With 64 illustrations. 8vo, $2.00

"The following legends," says Mr. Stanley in his introduction, "are the choicest and most curious of those that were related to me during seventeen years, and which have not been hitherto published in any of my books of travel." There are in all nineteen stories, new and striking in motive and quaint in language.

MY KALULU.

Prince, King, and Slave. A Story of Central Africa. By HENRY M. STANLEY. One volume, 12mo, new edition, with many illustrations, $1.50.

HENRY M. STANLEY.

"A fresh, breezy, stirring story for youths, interesting in itself and full of information regarding life in the interior of the continent in which its scenes are laid."—NEW YORK TIMES.

"If the young reader is fond of strange adventures, he will find enough in this volume to delight him all winter, and he will be hard to please who is not charmed by its graphic pages."—BOSTON JOURNAL.

Jules Verne's Greatest Work.

"THE EXPLORATION OF THE WORLD."

"M. Verne's scheme in this work is to tell fully how man has made acquaintance with the world in which he lives, to combine into a single work in three volumes the wonderful stories of all the great explorers, navigators, and travelers who have sought out, one after another, the once uttermost parts of the earth."—THE NEW YORK EVENING POST.

The three volumes in a set, $7.50; singly, $2.50.

FAMOUS TRAVELS AND TRAVELLERS.

With over 100 full-page illustrations, maps, etc., 8vo, $2.50.

THE GREAT NAVIGATORS OF THE XVIIITH CENTURY.

With 96 full-page illustrations and 19 maps, 8vo, $2.50.

THE GREAT EXPLORERS OF THE XIXTH CENTURY.

With over 100 full-page illustrations, fac-similes, etc., 8vo, $2.50.

Jules Verne's Stories.   Uniform Illustrated Edition.

Nine volumes, 8vo, extra cloth, with over 750 full-page illustrations. Price, per set, in a box, $17.50.   Sold also in separate volumes.

MICHAEL STROGOFF; or, The Courier of the Czar, $2.00. A FLOATING CITY AND THE BLOCKADE RUNNERS, $2.00. HECTOR SERVADAC, $2.00. A JOURNEY TO THE CENTRE OF THE EARTH, $2.00. FROM THE EARTH TO THE MOON DIRECT IN NINETY-SEVEN HOURS, TWENTY MINUTES; AND A JOURNEY AROUND IT, $2.00. DICK SANDS, $2.00. THE STEAM HOUSE, $2.00. THE GIANT RAFT, $2.00. THE MYSTERIOUS ISLAND, $2.50.

S. P. Henderson,
Dec. 25th 1892 -

P9-CMM-642